Curvy Girls Do It Collection
9 Complete Erotic Romance Stories

**Curvy Girls Do It Collection: 9 Complete
Erotic Romance Stories**

By

Ulriche Kacey Padraige

9 Complete Erotic Romance Stories

Curvy Girls Do It Collection
9 Complete Erotic Romance Stories

Enjoy all the Curvy Girls Do It Erotic Romance Stories in one bundle, with a special bonus story - **Curvy Girls Do It at Graduation Party.**

Please keep this book away from minors

Curvy Girls Do It Deeper

The Curvy Girls

Curvy girls do it deeper. That's the tagline to our online presence – well, the fact is that this book will reach out to the geographical area where we live so we are not going to mention the town where we live.

We would if we were not already busy enough with the guys here. The point of this book is to tell you about how we solved a problem that every woman has. We cannot get enough sex.

Yes, you heard me right. We cannot get enough sex. I really should be putting that in the past tense. We get enough sex now.

This story is being told by all three of us but we are just going to use the first person to tell the story. It doesn't matter which one of us tells the story because for all of us the story is the same.

Our Story

We were in graduate school when this started. Well, Amy and Amanda were. Beth was already graduated and working. Even though she works for a major bank, she had the same problem that Amy and Amanda had.

All three of us were horny, horny, horny. Our first thought was to join a dating site to meet men for casual encounters. Hmm. That did not turn out all that well. Most of them wanted to get into a serious committed relationship.

There are dating sites that are really just meet-up sites and we tried those. Too many married men. Married men want to meet weird hours like at midnight when their wives go to work the midnight shift. Or they keep cancelling because they cannot get away.

Ah, this is all nonsense talking about what we didn't want. What we did want was sex, lots of sex, and good sex. However, we were very very busy and the bar scene just didn't work.

That is nothing more than ending up with some guy who's had too much to drink. In spite of what men think, booze does not turn them into handsome, sexy creatures that are capable of imaginative sex.

We don't have open schedules and the time to get into all the surrounding palaver that goes with the dating and pick up scene.

We wanted free access to open and unbridled sex when we needed it and had time available.

Some people might say that this is a man's approach to sex – we want what we want when we want it.

Let's Be Honest
Wanting sex when we want it and how we want it is what it is all about. I don't know if all women are like this and just hide their desire and needs or if there is something about the dedication to our work

and study lives that made us feel the way we feel. We vibrate with currents of sexual energy that runs through us.

You don't know how many times I had to slide my hand into my panties in my study carrel and just bring myself to a gasping orgasm. I mean, three times a day sometimes I had to do this. It's distracting and time-consuming. And for Beth, it was really difficult.

Beth works in an office and usually her colleagues just tap on the door and then open it and come in to ask her about a file or some such thing and she can't be there with her face in orgasmic bliss and her fingers twiddling her swollen clit, now can she?

The Look of Us

It's a fact that people really don't know how to describe themselves properly. For one thing, people really cannot see themselves entirely. For instance, what does your ass look like? Or the back of your head.

I suppose you could hold up a mirror and describe these things. But the real problem is that we find it difficult to be blunt and accurate about our appearance. We see flaws where there are no flaws just a human feature.

So what we did was we got one of the other girls to describe us here. The deal is that we are not allowed to change the description that she wrote. Amy described Beth and Beth described Amanda and – you guessed it – Amanda described Amy.

Beth

Beth is five feet seven inches tall. She has streaked blonde hair in a pageboy crop. Her legs are long and her hips are narrow. When she is in a skirt, she looks like she has no ass at all but she does. It is tiny and rounded with each buttock firm and perky. When I look at Beth's ass, the phrase that comes to mind is "lift and separate."

Her skin is pale and she never bothers trying to tan. She thinks tanning is not healthy for skin. Her bones seem to be long and slender. Over the round buttocks, she has a smoothly indented waist and a long lean torso with tiny tits.

Her breasts barely rise off her chest, she is so flat, but her nipples are outstanding. They are dark and stand out a good inch even when they are at rest. When she is aroused, they seem to double in size.

Beth has a long slender neck and a sweet face. While her entire body is sleek and graceful, her face is mobile and elastic. Her mouth can be tiny and pursed or spread in the widest smile you ever imagine. Her eyes are a startling green and her eyebrows are gently arched and a light brown color.

Amy

Amy is five feet three inches tall and she is rounded. Her legs are shapely, tiny ankles, curvaceous calves and thighs. Full broad and round bum. Her waist does not dip but leads almost straight from hip to chest.

She is a double-D cup girl with huge breasts. Her nipples are big and pale pink. Even when she is fully aroused, they don't get big and hard but the aureole turns a deeper pink. Amy has a classic beauty. Her cheeks are dimpled and she has masses of curly black hair that she lets fly loose around her shoulders.

Amy's eyes are a deep dark brown and her skin has a dusky olive tint.

Amanda

Amanda is built like a tomboy and loves to wear oversized clothes. She's five feet five inches tall and completely toned and muscular. I don't mean she has big bulging muscles but she is sleek and smoothly muscled.

Her eyes are hazel with dark lashes. Her eyebrows are also dark and dramatic. She has a sprinkling of little freckles over her nose. She keeps her ash brown hair trimmed in a pixie cut.

Her breasts are firm and make a good handful. They do not droop at all. She has a curvy shape and her thighs look like they are sculptured. So does her ass.

Now You Know Us – Kind Of

So there you have it – we are friends, we are smart and educated, we're not bad looking, and we're horny. Put this all together and we brainstormed the perfect solution to wanting good sex, when we want it and how we want it.

The Curvy Girls Club

We created the curvy girls club. The club meets when we want it to meet – usually around 10 p.m. We have a small group that we invite and they can come if they are available. If they are already busy for the evening, there's no penalty for not coming.

It started out with each of us inviting a guy that we thought would be fun to play with. We picked Beth's house for the club meeting place because it has the space we need. It's a three-bedroom house with a den that can be converted into a bedroom pretty quickly.

The three of us kept on thinking about the club and refined it as we went. It's been our source of fun for almost two years by now and we love it. Here are some of the refinements that we came up with.

The guys have to be open-minded. This is necessary because if only two guys show up, they have to service all three of us. If six guys show up, we have to service all six of them. You can see that the guys have to know that this is for fun and no one owns anyone.

The guys have to have big cocks. Sometimes we have new guests and they are not as well equipped as we like and we just don't add them to the ongoing list unless they have other amazing skills.

Part of this is because, well, we like big thick cocks. The other thing is, guys with small cocks tend to get upset and competitive if they are surrounded by well-hung men.

We have a list of a couple of dozen men on the ongoing list and we text them in batches of six...we just mention the time and say, hope to see you there. The next night, we text the next six. Sometimes one of us is busy with or has something else to do. Those nights, the other two might send out a text to only four of the guys.

They usually reply to say if they will be there, sometimes they cannot say for sure. It's fairly informal. The guys like us and we have a lot of fun together even though we barely actually talk to each other.

We were going to tell you about our favorite guys but they are all our favorites so we decided to let five of the guys tell you about the fun we have together.

Matt

Matt is a businessman who plays squash and golfs. He keeps himself in decent shape although he is forty, or at least admits to being forty. He might be a bit older but he can easily pass for under forty so we don't care if he is vain about his age.

He's divorced and was in a couple of unsuccessful romances so this arrangement suits him well. Matt is compact. He's about five feet seven and keeps his dark hair in a short crew cut.

Here's what Matt thinks of us.

I first met Beth through work and was attracted to her. She looked so cool and collected in her pale green linen suit. I was just out of a bad relationship and debated asking Beth out for a drink.

If she was as cool in person as she appeared to be, I figured it would be great because I was not interested in getting involved in another relationship. Not for a while, anyway. After seeing her in a work situation several times, I took a chance and suggested that we have a drink after the seminar we were both attending.

She agreed and over drinks we chatted about life. She surprised me by bringing it up first – the mechanics of having fun without commitment. I can still see her face, staring me straight in the eye, as she said, "My friends and I like to have fun, lots and lots of fun, but it has to be completely without strings."

What guy can resist following up on a lead like that?

Not this one, that is for sure.

She invited me to her house to meet her friends the next evening. It was very strange. Her house is lovely and decorated in stark colors. Amy and Amanda were there and both as beautiful as any women I have ever met. However, my predilection is for slim blondes.

I have to make it clear, I have had sex with all sorts of women but my turn-on is the Beth type. Somehow the three women managed to get me to open up and tell them that. They then led me into Beth's bedroom and all three of them undressed me.

I was standing there naked and Beth took my face in her hands and kissed me a long hard kiss. While she was doing that, Amanda began massaging my ass and reached between my thighs and lifted my balls in her hand.

Amy had her hands between me and Beth and took my penis in one of her hands and gave me long slow strokes.

Do you have any idea what it is like to have three women, six hands playing with your body? All I can say is that once we were all four of us in bed, I had no idea whose lips were wrapped around my cock or whose nipple I was sucking.

It was a thrust party, plunging from one pussy to the next, hands on two sets of tits and my face buried in the set of boobs in the middle. Then Amy slid out of the pack of women and shortly after she was followed by Amanda, leaving me alone with Beth.

It almost felt kinky to mount her in the missionary style, clutching her tight ass close to me as I drove my cock deep inside her, over and over again. She arched her back up so that she could accommodate my full length.

I read the first part of this story so I know that you already know that the curvy girls like their men with big dicks. So I'm not telling you anything that you already don't know when I tell you that I have a ten-incher.

It's a great topic in the locker room but in reality, most women, especially after you are in a relationship with them, find it hard to real fuck a dick that long. It hurts, they say or there are positions that they don't like because it hits the end of their vagina.

Beth not only was soaking wet, she loved the deeper I went into her. I think her g-spot is way way back in that magic cunt of hers. She reached over her head and grabbed the headboard so she was lifted entirely off the bed, her legs wrapped around me as I rode her to orgasm after orgasm.

She stopped me before I dropped my load in her and rotated so I was behind her. This is a well-known position for really deep penetration. She told me to fuck her as hard as I wanted to.

So I did. This was a rare treat for me. Most women didn't like to have me pound them from behind but Beth loves it. I drove the full ten inches into her over and over and that was how I finished, that first night.

I have been back to Beth's place numerous times. Often there are three of us men there and all three women and I have time alone with Beth. But the fact is, it doesn't matter that much. I like all three women.

The "anything goes" atmosphere is outstanding. Once Beth caught on to the joy I felt in fucking her from behind, she asked me if I was interested in anal sex. I had never tried it. Let's face it, not every woman likes anal sex and even those who do are not interested in taking it up the ass from someone with a big cock.

I hemmed and hawed in answering and then she asked if I had ever had sex that way and I gave her the usual reply, "Not as a recipient."

She tapped me lightly with a slap on my wrist. "In other words, no," she said.

Then she explained that Amy loved taking it up the ass and size did not bother her. "It's like she is a sword swallower in reverse," Beth explained.

The next thing I knew, there I was, poised over Amy's round ass, with Beth lubricating my cock while Amanda lubricated Amy's hole. The two of them guided me into the warm dark spot and the feeling was like nothing I had ever experienced before. It was hot and tight, gripping the base of my cock tighter than I had ever felt before.

I pushed in and then pulled back nearly to the opening and let it slide slowly full length back in, over and over. The feeling was so intense, the nerves all along my spinal cord were tingling.

Amy said, "Harder."

And I began driving myself into her slamming my pelvis against her big soft ass. Then I reached around and massaged and squeezed her bit tits while I rode to the biggest and most intense orgasm of my life.

Oh yes, these curvy girls do it deeper.

Zev

Zev is intense and wiry but quite tall – well over six feet. He has short curly black hair and intense brown eyes and the thickest cock any of us have ever seen. It's probably not much more than eight inches long but none of us can close our hands around it. The only way we can blow him is to have one of us lick the head of his cock while the other two manipulate his shaft.

Amy brought him into the curvy girl circle. He is a medical student and works long and intense hours. He was complaining to one of his buddies who is in the same seminar course that Amy is in.

Zev told his friend he would dearly love to have a good screw but he didn't have the time or energy to talk to anyone before or after. They were talking while waiting for the elevator.

Amy went up to him before the elevator arrived and invited him over to the house that evening. She said, just drop by, here's the address and wrote it down on a piece of paper and handed it to him. Zev grinned at her and said he would see what he could do.

Here's what Zev thinks of us.

When Amy invited me over to the house, I was sure that she was like most of the women I met. She would pretend to understand that I didn't have time for a social life but after a couple of dates that would change.

"You are just using me for sex, blah blah blah."

I could not have been more wrong.

I did show up at the house that night. I was so horny I would have screwed a snake and the thought that I might be getting laid that night had me wondering if I shouldn't jerk off just to take off the edge before I got out of my car.

It's a good thing I didn't. When I got there, there were a couple of other guys already there and of course, Beth and Amanda. We all were introduced and then the girls laid it out for me. Everyone was busy and it was all about having fun.

We were in the living room and Amy was the first one to strip naked. Then the rest of us followed. I kind of assumed I would be with Amy since she was the one who invited me but it was hard to tell how the pairings were supposed to take place.

One of the other men said that he didn't play with men and the girls laughed and said that they all did so he didn't have too. Amy sucked on one guy's cock, just a lick or two and then she looked over at me and said, oh wow, that's what I want and she put her hand around my dick and led me into a bedroom.

Shortly I heard the others pair off and I could feel my cock throbbing. I wondered if I would make it past the first stroke. Amy pushed me gently, so that I was lying on my back on the bed. She was kneeling over me with her big tits just about in my face.

I grabbed both of them and mashed them together.

"Suck my tits," she breathed into my ear and hoisted herself up over my cock so that I could feel the wetness. I was smothered in boobs and sucking and nibbling on her massive titties when she shoved herself down over me, gasping as she did so.

"Oh, you're ready to go, aren't you," she said and began to bounce energetically up and down on my throbbing penis. I shot my load deep into her and she kept on bouncing, moaning as she climaxed several times.

She stayed on top of me and asked if I was in a rush to leave or did I want to recuperate and have more fun. I should have been in a hurry but I wanted more. This was the first time in months I'd had sex or even masturbated. I had a taste of it and thirty seconds was hardly more than enough to wet my whistle.

I told her I wanted more. She took me with her to the kitchen where we had a glass of water and then she led me to a bedroom where Amanda and this big blond guy were fucking.

It was amazing how Amy did it but she slid into the bed next to Amanda and reached over to the guy and brought his hands over to her tits. "Come over here, big boy," she said. She looked at me and saw that my prick was as hard again as ever and she said, "Get over here Zev and show Amanda what you have. She'll love it."

The next thing I knew I had Amanda's ankles around my neck and was pushing myself into her pussy, which was open and ready, already lubricated and stretched by the blond guy.

The four of us fucked side by side for a good half hour, each of us changing positions and sucking and biting and pounding. It was the first time ever in my life that I felt that I would get all the tail I needed without that tense feeling that it would all be over long before I was ready to call it a night.

After I came inside Amanda, the blond guy indicated that he would like another shot at her and I pulled out and rolled out of the way so he could have her.

And he did. My cock didn't even go down after my orgasm and I raised my eyebrows to ask Amy if I could have some more and she nodded.

For the next half hour, blondie and me took turns screwing these two gorgeous women. I am not sure how it was for him but each time I felt that I was going to shoot again, I would tap his shoulder and we would swap places.

I remember his cock was very long but not as thick as mine. A lot longer but not as thick. Those girls are amazing. They love to fuck and the constant switch from cock to cock made the experience amazingly intense.

Finally I couldn't stand it any more. I had to come and come soon. That's when Beth showed up. I was moving from Amanda to Amy when she came in the room. She reached out and took my cock in her hand.

"Come with me," she said. Meanwhile her partner was with her and he stepped in (or slid in) where I had been and when I left the room, he was pumping into Amy.

Beth took me to her room and rubbed her little tits all over with the head of my cock, then she pulled me down and rolled me over and straddled me, squatting slowly down over my hard penis. She slid up and down and then settled down to absorb all of me. Her cunt was hot and tight and it enveloped me like a tight glove.

I grabbed her hips and held her tight to me while I thrust up into her until I exploded in my third orgasm of the night.

I'm still a regular with the curvy girls. How could I go back to regular boring old game-playing sex after having a taste of these three luscious babes?

Wendell

Wendell was a visiting professor who was a proper British man with an Oxford accent and tweed blazers. He was so buttoned down that we actually just invited him over to Beth's for dinner. The course was over and he was heading back to England. It seemed like the least we could do, invite him over for an evening of social entertainment.

We had several glasses of wine with dinner and then after dinner, we were sipping brandy and Beth said that she had almost forgotten how to have a conversation. Wendell expressed surprise and said that he imagined that we entertained a lot. Amanda gets giggly when she drinks and she said, "Oh yes, we do but not the talking kind of entertaining."

Wendell became very interested. Amy refilled the brandy snifters and gave a little detail about what we considered entertaining.

Amanda blurted out, "We love to fuck."

Here's what Wendell thinks of us.

I still gasp when I think of that night. Here I am sitting there with three very clever ladies, talking about music and literature and suddenly one of them announces that she likes to fuck.

The next thing I know, I admit that I have the same inclinations toward pleasure but it was a difficult position to be in, teaching and the only women I met were students or a few colleagues and it was not appropriate to become intimate with any of them.

Amanda pointed out that there were no students of his or colleagues either in the room. She suggested that we all undress and see what happens. The next thing I know, yes I am repeating myself but that was the way the whole evening was, the next thing I know, I am in a bedroom with three lovely ladies attending to my sensual needs. One was brushing her huge breasts all over my face while another one was sucking my penis and the third one placed my available hand on her pubic mound.

I had not had sex for several months and self-satisfaction only takes a person so far. They were doing things to me that I had never had done before. I was covered in woman-flesh. They were licking in places that had never been touched before except by the spray from my shower nozzle.

They were doing things to my testicles that were unheard of in my world. Finally, they placed me in the old-fashioned man on top position over Beth and guided my penis into her warm wet slit.

I was in town for another few days and I went back to visit them twice more and we played this game again with minor variations.

Trent

Trent was another one of Amy's friends that she brought home with her. He had gone through his undergraduate program on an athletic scholarship and he is huge. His hands can almost wrap entirely around a football. He is African-American and his skin glows almost purple, it's so dark.

He has an amazing cock, thick and long and heavily veined. It is a work of art. He's in graduate school now and chose not to pursue a career in football after

he graduated with his first degree. He didn't think
that it would be a suitable long-term career for him.

He and Amy became friends and when he broke up
with his girlfriend, or more accurately, when she
broke up with him, he was crushed.

Amy listened to him talk about how he felt while
they walked to the library. One day he said that he
knew the best thing was to get back on the horse
again, after falling off. But, he confided, He was too
busy and too into his studies to really have the time
to start dating again.

"I'm a man in transition," he told her.

Amy sat him down and told him about the curvy
girls. "We love sex but we don't love games and bull
shit."

Here's what Trent thinks of us.

I've never seen anything like those ladies. When I
feel horny, I check to see if they texted me and
sometimes Amy has. She'll say, look they others are

busy tonight. Why don't you come on over here to my place?

She and Amanda share a little apartment but they each have their own bedroom. Amy's got this little bed. It's a double bed, I guess, but I'm six feet seven inches tall. I barely fit in the bed by myself.

Other times, a couple of them will have me over at Beth's and, my favorite is when all three of them are there at Beth's. I mean, I'm a man who needs a lot of pussy and they can provide that.

We have a routine, when it's all three of us. We all get into Beth's big bed and into a huddle of flesh. I cannot get enough breasts and I loved to suck on Beth's long hard nipples and squeeze Amy's big round boobs at the same time. If I'm really lucky, I get to have Amy's tits in one hand and Amanda's in the other while sucking on Beth's nipples.

Whichever one I'm fucking, the other two shove their boobs at me. I can chew and nibble from breast to breast, moving from one to the other and back again. They're agile girls, for sure, and we have this thing going where I can plunge into one and then quickly pull out and plunge into another.

Sometimes there are other guys there too and on those nights, I pretty much stick to Amy. Well, she's the one who is mostly my friend and she does have lovely breasts.

I like to spoon with her and slide my cock deep inside her from behind. I can finger her asshole while I am probing her pussy. It's cozy and loving and very satisfying.

Best of all, there is no hassle. If I found someone I wanted to date, I'd just stop coming by and they would wish me well. The best part is that by not being horny all the time, I never confuse my real feelings with that hunger that can get into your heart and under your skin.

Armand

Most of the men that we have on our party list (for lack of a better name) are into the usual types of sex. Some like to get into their favorite position and let their imaginations run wild. Every now and then we meet someone with special interests. Armand is one of these guys. He's in his mid-thirties but he looks a lot older. It's like he was born old.

Armand likes to be spanked. He likes a good firm spanking, preferably with a leather belt. He is adequately endowed but he's not interested in anything other than being spanked and he can achieve orgasm only this way.

The thing is, the whole point of this sex game that we love so much is that all three of us love having a big hard cock pressed into us. We need multiple orgasms and we need men who can provide these to us on a regular basis.

Armand is a widower. His loneliness is so apparent and he helped Amanda out of a bind once – did I mention that he is a lawyer? We like Armand and since we usually have multiple visitors of a session, and since it pleases Armand, and to be completely honest, Beth enjoys spanking him. She makes jokes about it but I see the sparkle in her eyes when she is wielding the strap.

Amy doesn't use the strap too vigorously. She is a soft-hearted person and does not like to give anyone pain. Amanda is kind of in the middle. Therefore, we usually let Beth do the strapping.

Here's what Armand thinks of us.

After my wife died, I thought I would die too of sheer loneliness. She understood my special needs in the bedroom and while we did have traditional sex in the beginning, neither of us was all that interested.

I know there are specialists who are into providing that kind of sexual satisfaction. But there is something about paying for it that takes it into the area of too much humiliation. The girls hinted that they were willing to help me with my problem.

I know they like sex, and lots of it, and sometime they have other men there when I am there but that is a kind of perverse pleasure in hearing these men have intercourse in the next room while Beth paddle my behind.

One night Amy came into the room while Beth was applying the leather to me and she reached under me and squeezed my penis and at that moment, I experienced an immense orgasm.

I feel so safe with these women and love the sexual sounds and smells that surround me at Beth's place.

Summary

It might sound like we are exhausted with all this socializing and you might be thinking that if we spend all this time with all these men, we might as well be on the dating scene. The reality is that we do spend a couple of hours four or five nights a week but we do it when we want. There are no hassles with men trying to work out complicated arrangements or jealousies.

If we want to stop seeing any of these men, we just take them off our party list. But why would we want to? The interesting thing is lately, we think Beth is developing real feeling for Armand. And if that happens, then that happens.

Amy and Amanda were thinking about talking to Beth about us all moving in together in her house but when we saw a glimmer of this fondness that

Beth has for Armand, it made us stop and think about how we need to let things unfold as they should. Amanda said that she could see Beth marrying Armand and yet keep on playing the sex games we play.

"He'd love it. He could do the housework and clean up after us and do the laundry and she could spank him and he would love it," Amy said.

The stories here are from some of the guys that we have been having fun with for the last year and more. Some of the other guys were part of the games for months but they drifted away. Some moved to other cities.

A couple of them got into serious relationships but I have a feeling they will be back. One man fell in love with Amy and he had to go. We were afraid he would turn into some kind of stalker.

Our work lives have been tremendous since we found this way to enjoy the things in life that we really like. Our minds are clear. By the time we sleep after a couple of raucous hours of sex (and have sent the men home), we are bright-eyed and eager to plunge into our studies and our work. Our bodies are tingling and fine-tuned. Life is good.

Things might change down the road. For instance, next year when Amy and Amanda finish graduate school, one or both of us might move to another city. A lot of things can happen but we live in the moment. There is no need to think about these things now.

Right now, it is all about the curvy girls getting the sex that they need and getting their work underway done to the best of their abilities.

Curvy Girls Do It Pregnant and Horny

What's a Girl to Do?

When Carrie Ann realized she was pregnant, she was ecstatic. This was part of her very organized plan for her life. She would have a child. It was a planned pregnancy and she felt ever so slightly risqué in not even asking for the ultrasound information on whether it was a boy or a girl.

Carrie Ann read the books and watched the videos and researched pregnancy and motherhood online. There was very little that she did not know about the changes in her body that were taking place on a daily basis.

She was six months along. Standing in front of the full length mirror in her bedroom, she surveyed her body. Her ankles were still slim curving up to shapely calves. Her thighs were still smooth and from a direct front angle, her hips were narrow.

Then, there was her belly.

It was round and high and shiny-smooth. Her navel was a round button right in the center of the rounded belly. It curved down in a smooth curve to her pubic hair.

She used to keep her bush neatly trimmed with a narrow strip of dark hair that looked like an exclamation mark just above her slit.

Her skin was a smooth pale brown with a slightly pinkish tinge and the dark strip of public hair was a nice touch, she used to think.

However, the bigger her belly got, the more difficult it was to keep her pubes neatly manicured. So she had let her fur grow wild.

Now she had a great big thick thatch of brown hair, kind of auburn, under her big belly.

She knew she could easily head to the salon and have a wax session and her twat would be as smooth as ever but she didn't want to.

Right now, looking like this was suiting her just fine and dandy. She liked her mother earth look.

Her breasts were huge. Bigger than they had ever been. Looking at them gave her a twinge in her vagina. She lifted her hands to them and felt their roundness and fullness.

Her nipples had always been flat and pink, dark pink, but pink surrounded by a wide aureole. Now they were standing up looking like pencil erasers, both in color and size.

She tweaked her nipples and felt a tightness grip her clit as if there was a direct strand of nerves running from her nipples to her clit, a double strand each one leading to her nub of passion.

Her face was smooth and unlined and full of smiles. Smiles in her eyes and on her mouth.

She was happy.

But she was horny.

There was an irony to being fertile and pregnant, something that had happened with clinical precision, because it was done in a clinic.

Carrie Ann liked her life simple and uncomplicated. Sex was the same thing. It should be simple and uncomplicated. She had always had a fuck buddy in her life and sometimes the guy was more than just someone to have sexual fun with.

However, no one ever struck her with such passion that she wanted to spend the rest of her life with him. Certainly there was no one she wanted to have as part of her child's life.

Since she needed a sperm donor, she did the best thing she could think of and found just that, a sperm donor who was completely anonymous.

She had managed to create a lifestyle for herself that allowed her to provide a great home for herself and the future. She worked from home so that she could be a mother to her child as the child grew up.

Life was perfect.

Except for one thing.

She was horny.

Carrie Ann's horniness was not the usual aching that she used to get, where she wanted to feel a big thick cock sliding into her honey hole.

This was a deep throbbing urge that was almost painful. She tried relieving the pressure with her trusty purple vibrator and the orgasm was fast and intense but it did not quench her lust.

Five minutes later, the emptiness was like a wound inside her. It was located deep inside her pussy, like a greedy grasping hand reaching for a cock that would glide the full length of her snatch over and over and over until she melted in a body-shattering orgasm.

What's a girl to do? She needed sex and she needed a lot of it. She was hoping that the lust was something like morning sickness that would go away but it seemed to get more intense.

Getting Advice

Beth was one of Carrie Ann's best friends. Beth was one of those people that are unflappable and unshockable. She also had a great circle of friends and Carrie Ann knew that some of Beth's friends were into social sexual activities. She would be the go-to person for a topic such as this. Such as where does a girl go to when she is so horny that doorknobs look good to her?

But she is beyond being a curvy girl. She is a mountain of a woman with curves that are like the Rockies and a desire that is even bigger.

In this case, a girl calls Beth.

She invited Beth for lunch. Beth breezed in just after noon and they sipped Perrier water with lemon slices and ate Greek salad that Carrie Ann had tossed together.

Beth was looking as cool and limber as usual and she enthused over Carrie Ann's healthy appearance and patted her belly.

Then Carrie Ann got down to business. She loved the freedom she felt when she talked to Beth about sexual things. She jumped right in to the topic that was on her mind.

"It's like this, Beth. I need to get laid." Carrie Ann grinned. "And I need it bad."

Beth laughed. "Oh you are so funny. You make it sound like a big chore. You're gorgeous."

Carrie Ann waved her hands over her belly and said, "But look at this."

"There are men out there who would give their eye teeth to have sex with someone as pregnant as you are." Then Beth went on to tell Carrie Ann about one of her friends, a guy named Harold who dreamed about having sex with someone in labor.

"Nothing give Harold a bigger boner than just talking about the sensation of mounting a woman who is bursting with pregnancy."

The problem is, Beth went on, that there are not a lot of pregnant women in Beth's circle of friends and the ones who are pregnant are typically married and not interested in playing.

Carrie Ann knew that Beth and a couple of her girlfriends were into some serious sex parties. She had even gone to one before she was pregnant.

That was a lot of fun, she remembered. The Curvy Girls, they called themselves. Beth, Amy and Amanda. They were not overly curvy. Carrie Ann knew women who used "curvy" as a euphemism for fat.

Beth, Amy and Amanda were not fat. They were well curved, well Beth was kind of long and lean, but the others were fuller in the hips and breast than Beth was.

However, all three of them were bent and they liked the notation of curvy for their sexual pleasures because it referred to their gentle bent nature.

Don't Want Perverts!

The big phrase that kept popping up was "We don't want perverts." The first time that Beth told Carrie Ann about their house parties, Carrie Ann blurted out, "but what about pervs?"

Well, there are no pervs in Beth's world. Carrie Ann found that out on her visit to one of Beth's parties.

Beth was still smiling when she told Carrie Ann that she would invite Harold over Friday night if Carrie Ann was interested.

And she assured Carrie Ann that Harold was anything but a perv. Carrie Ann grinned back. She was not as adventuresome as Beth but she was expanding her social skills to encompass some daring new ventures.

Three years ago, she never would have imagined that she would be having a baby on her own. She also would not have believed that she would be as horny as she was right now.

Just knowing that she was going to get fucked Friday night made her damp.

After Beth went back to work, Carrie Ann went to bed with her dildo. She took a pair of old-fashioned wooden clothes pins, the kind with the spring near the bottom, and clipped them on her pointed nipples.

The exquisite pleasure of the nipple clamps almost brought her to orgasm when she walked to the dresser to get her dildo. Her pussy lips were swollen, engorged with blood, and the pressure of them on her clitoris which was peeping out from between her lips made her tingle.

It was swollen and distended, caught between her labia. When Carrie Ann laid herself down on the bed, she stroked her fingers along her slit and felt her wetness.

She turned on the vibrating dildo and let it graze her clit, feeling the shooting tingles that meant she was about two strokes from a gasping climax.

She spread her legs and lifted her hips and thrust the dildo into her vagina. It pulsed and twitched and she felt her juices run down her crack to the bed.

When she could stand it no longer, she slid the slick dildo up to her slit and held it lightly against her tiny dick-like nub.

It was like ice and fire at the same time, waves of pleasure starting in her core and reaching to her head and feet as she bounced her hips eagerly against her mechanical penis, pressing her clit hungrily against it.

She collapsed in a drenched heap on her bed, clothes pins still on her nipples and drifted into a sleep, the dildo, vibration turned off, resting in her pubic hair.

The relief was more satisfying than the last few times she had done herself but she still had to repeat this self-gratification ritual a few more times before Friday night. It took the edge off in one way but it made her more powerfully aware of her need to feel a man's body against hers.

To feel a man's cock inside her.

A Needy Bunch

Carrie Ann parked her car and looked at Beth's house. It was elegant and modern at the same time.

The door opened before she even got to the front step and Beth ushered her in.

The men were not there yet but Amy and Amanda were. They exchanged hugs and greetings. Carrie Ann knew that usually the women shared the men when they had an evening together and sometimes there were more than three men for the three women to play with.

They wanted to discuss this with Carrie Ann before the men arrived. Harold was coming they assured her but perhaps some of the other men might like her special aura of pregnancy.

The events of the evening, they assured her, were entirely up to her.

"You only need to go as far as you want with Harold," Amy said. "He understands that."

Amanda added, "But if you are interested in more action, I know that at least one of the others interested."

Carrie Ann thought she would burst with horniness. She said, in all honesty, "I could take all of them all night long."

Beth said, "Well that is good to hear because we are planning to make this a long session. One of the guys is a chef and he has plans to make us brunch in the morning."

"This is a needy bunch coming tonight," Amanda said. "There are five of them. Harold and four others."

"Do you still have the same – uh, requirements?" Carrie Ann asked.

They had told her that the men had to be healthy, and certified healthy, and they had to have huge cocks.

Harold was there first. Carrie Ann liked him immediately. He was a gentle person, she could tell, but extremely handsome. Sculpted cheeks, thick blond hair, startlingly blue eyes.

His arms were bulky with muscles and his ass was high and rounded. She could see that through the tailored wool slacks he was wearing.

Beth had provided Harold and Carrie Ann with the bigger of the spare bedrooms and thoughtfully placed a stack of pillows on the cozy chair to the right of the bed.

Harold and Carrie Ann held hands as they entered the bedroom and Carrie Ann could feel that his hand was trembling.

She sat on the edge of the bed and looked up at him, still holding his hand.

"May I?" he asked, indicating that he wanted to put his hands on her belly.

She nodded. He was still standing and bent forward so that he could place a hand on either side of her protuberance. The feel of someone else's hands on her swollen stomach made Carrie Ann moan.

It was a very low moan but it encouraged Harold who knelt down in front of her. He pressed his lips against her belly and then gently lifted her top and pulled the stretchy waist band of her pants down so that her entire belly was exposed.

He kissed her belly and stroked it.

"You are beautiful," he murmured.

He lifted her feet up and rearranged her on the bed, pulling her pants and undies down over her hips and knees and ankles.

"Oh," he exclaimed. "I love your big hairy bush." His voice caught on his words. His excitement was palpable.

He unsnapped her bra and removed her top. It was his turn to moan when he saw her full firm breasts.

He knelt over her on the bed, taking a nipple in his lips and teeth, nibbling gently.

Carrie Ann was almost dizzy with desire, with the thrill of having her nipples nibbled but she wanted them sucked and sucked hard. She pushed her chest up and said, "Harder. Harder."

Harold took one breast between his hands and sucked the nipple entirely into his mouth and sucked, using his tongue trapping her swollen nipple against the roof of his mouth.

He slid his mouth to the other breast and gave it the same attention holding it immobile with one hand, while he twisted and twirled the exposed nipple with his free hand.

He stopped long enough to remove his clothes and returned to her breasts. Carrie Ann could feel his long hard cock pressing against the side of her belly.

Harold moved so that he was between her legs and asked if she were all right. She nodded yes. He swept his hands down over her belly and took the cheeks of her ass one in each large hand and lifted her up as he moved his head down between her legs.

He licked gently along her slit, stopping to take her clit between his teeth and sucked on it as he had sucked on her nipples.

She began to cum, pressing herself against his face. She moaned and cried out as he sucked her, feeling her juices squirt against his chin.

"Fuck me," she cried.

His cock was so hard, it was throbbing and bouncing, almost painful. He moved up, kissing her belly and feeling the baby roll in her stomach, the little body making her skin ripple as it turned around inside her.

The power of his need to possess her body almost took his breath away. He moved up over her belly, his cock feeling the heat of her cunt against its head.

She moved urgently toward him, her hips thrusting against him and he felt the head of his cock move in to her warm wetness.

The pain of pushing his hardened cock into her was so intense, he both wanted it to end and to never end.

Once he was all the way in, as far as he could push himself, he lifted himself up to his knees and held his hands firmly at her waist, her belly huge against his and he pulled out, almost to the end and then pushed back in again, just as slowly as his first entrance.

"Are you all right?" he asked.

She moaned, "Yes. Oh yes. Fuck me. Hard."

He repeated the slow withdrawal and reentry several more times and then, holding her swollen belly between his hands, using his knees and thighs for power, he pounded his cock into her over and over and over.

She shrieked and moaned, writhing joyously against him. He felt her juices flowing. His cock was a mile long as he pressed into her as deep as he could.

He didn't want it to end just yet, he didn't want to stop fucking her.

When she slowed down to catch her breath, he slid out of her and guided her to roll over. She raised herself on her hands and knees and he positioned himself behind her, reaching around to wrap his arms fully around her body, feeling the weight of her pregnancy against his hands.

He knew that the excitement of this horny and pregnant woman might cause him to lose his load before he was all the way back in her but he had to try.

He ran his cock along the crack of her ass, stopping to push gently against her asshole before moving down to her dripping pussy.

He positioned the head of his cock at her opening and swiftly drove himself even further inside her. It was a matter of several strokes before he felt himself melt inside her.

After he unloaded his jism in her, he kept on thrusting for a few more minutes and then he had to stop. They lay side by side, his arms wrapped around her while they caught their breath.

Once is Not Enough

Harold said, "I wish I could do that again."

Carrie Ann laughed, "Me too."

"You like being fucked?" He laughed too. "Well, I guess that is pretty obvious."

"I feel like I have been starved so long that I never want this to stop."

"I can do it again but it will take maybe half an hour to get back up to speed." He looked at her, "I know that Ben would like to do you. How would you feel about that?"

"I'd love it."

He kissed her forehead. "I'll be right back."

He left the bedroom and a few minutes later, returned with Ben and George. Ben was tall and very thin, which made his man-meat look huge against his narrow hips. It was waving in front of him, moving up and down with each beat of his heart.

George was his exact opposite. He was short and broad shouldered, built like a wrestler. His cock was thick and dark against his curly black hair.

Harold had a warm face cloth and hand towel and he was washing Carrie Ann, as if she were a baby herself. He washed the juices from her slit and dried her. He stroked her hair and asked if she were ready for more.

He caressed her belly and was surprised that his prick was already bouncing back to action mode. He and George lifted her to the center of the bed and positioned themselves on one each side of her.

Ben arranged himself over her, his long arms and legs holding his body over her pregnancy, his cock drooling on her belly.

He rubbed his cock against her belly, gently and George and Harold each took a breast and like a pair of giant mismatched twins began suckling her tits while Ben moved his cock down between her legs.

"I have always wanted to do this," he said, as he pushed his cock into Carrie Ann. He rested his hands on her distended abdomen, and thrust into her again and again while the other two men kneaded her tits and sucked her nipples and ran their hands over her belly too.

They held her in their arms, wrapped fully around her, as Ben vibrated her body with his powerful thrusts into her eager pussy.

In Carrie Ann's blissful mind, she knew that she was finally having the sex that she wanted. She was enveloped in men.

She moaned and screamed and sighed. She opened her eyes and saw all three men over her. She reached for George cock and he followed her guidance and moved so that she could take him in her mouth.

She sucked mightily on his cock as Ben drenched her pussy with the second huge load of cum that night.

"I'm going to blow," George said.

Carrie Ann could not talk with her mouth full but she nodded.

She felt the first few drops of his cum in her mouth and then, she felt him pull it out of her mouth and let his load spray over her breasts and tummy.

In spite of three loads of cum in and on her, Carrie Ann was in a frenzy of passion and she knew that she could handle more fucking.

She was almost shy to ask for more and in her head she realized how ridiculous that was.

Harold asked her if she were all right again and she said, "I could do this all night."

Harold smiled at her, "So could I." His penis was rock hard again and he moved between her legs. Ben and George were sitting on the bed, one on either side of Carrie Ann, and they caressed her damp breasts and rubbed George's semen into her belly as Harold probed her wetness with his hard on.

When Carrie Ann finally slept, after another hour of passion with the three men, she slept more soundly than she ever had slept in her life.

When she woke in the morning, she was well rested but surprisingly horny all over again. She got out of bed and went into the en suite powder room and took a brisk hot shower.

Her twat was not sore but it was pleasantly tender. Her nipples were red and there were little signs of tender suckings on her breasts.

She was standing on the bathmat, pinching her own nipple when she heard the knock on the bedroom door.

"Come in," she said.

It was Harold. He had come to see how she was and when he saw her standing naked in the bathroom, he wanted her again.

She still had her fingers on her nipples. He walked toward her and knelt in front of her, his head at her breast level. He took her breasts in his hands and once again began to suck on them.

He knew what she liked and he drew long hard suck from each nipple, moving from one to the other.

"Do you want me to get one of the others, so both titties will be happy?" he asked.

"Yes. If you promise to fuck me again."

Harold chuckled and left her briefly. He came back with George. "Ben's making breakfast," Harold said. Then both men were in front of her, each one with a breast and each one of them with a hand on her ass cheeks.

As if they could read her mind, they picked her up in unison and carried her to the bed where they deposited her gently.

Harold took her first, laying the full weight of his body on hers. Once she made it clear that she liked this, he put his arms around her, pressing her breasts against his chest, and slowly and deliberately rode her with his erection deep inside her warm pussy, back and forth, back and forth, his stomach against hers, feeling the tautness of it, feeling the heat of her desire as she bucked and moaned against him.

He came, pumping his seed into her in waves of ecstasy. George simply watched, keeping an eye on her face to make sure that she was in no discomfort.

Seeing the blissful look as she came again and again, responding to Harold's powerful strokes, he felt himself filled with an urgent desire.

He stroked his cock and was thinking about bringing himself off when Carrie Ann opened her eyes and looked at him.

"I want some of that," she said with a big grin.

When Harold finally finished and moved out of Carrie Ann, she reached over for George and said, "I want to feel that cock in me now."

He moved over and took Harold's place. He felt the heat of Harold's semen as he wedged his cock into Carrie Ann's heated crevice.

9 Complete Erotic Romance Stories

In spite of the pounding she had just taken, she was snug and the feeling of her silken snatch sliding over his turgid cock was so satisfying, he could not believe it.

He felt her belly against his as he braced himself over her holding his weight off her with his arms.

She was thrusting against him before he was all the way inside her. He was so captivated by watching Harold fuck her that he realized almost immediately that he was not going to last long in this rhythmic pounding of this glorious girl.

And he didn't. He spilled his seed in gushes and thought it would never end as he drenched Carrie Ann's pussy with his orgasm.

Once More with Vigor

Breakfast was a chef's delight. The entire crew sat around and chatted and enjoyed the meal. When the men left a couple of hours later, the women did a recap of the night.

Carrie Ann tried to find the words to explain that she was temporarily replete. She felt a sense of well-being that she could not remember having ever felt before.

Her body hummed. In spite of the hours of fucking she had experienced, she felt surprisingly buoyant. No aching muscles. Her breasts were tender but they had been tender for several weeks anyway so she was not sure that the feeling in her breasts was from the new attention that had been paid to them or to the natural tenderness that apparently is part of pregnancy.

As she said good bye to Harold, separate from her good byes to the rest of the male guests, he asked if he could see her again.

It felt for a moment like high school and a shy boy asking for a second date.

"I have never had sex like that," he said. "I would hate to think that I will never have sex like that again."

Carrie Ann smiled and wrote down her phone number for him.

Thus began the sexual adventures that kept Carrie Ann satisfied for the rest of her pregnancy. Harold came to visit her at least twice a week and sometimes George and Ben came along too.

Twice George came on his own and once Ben came on his own.

While the four of them never all partied all night, or most of the night, like they did the first time, Carrie Ann never once felt that she was not getting enough sex.

Harold was extremely attentive and Carrie Ann noticed that as her pregnancy advanced he was with her more and more.

Beth dropped in to visit her at least once a week.

"You don't mind that the men come here, do you?" Carrie Ann asked Beth.

"Not at all," Beth patted her arm. "It's wonderful to see how happy they are with you. "Actually I'm a little jealous of the attention you are getting."

Carrie Ann did not tell Beth that the attention was likely to be short-lived. Her attraction for the men was due to her temporary state. Once she popped and the baby was born, her voluptuousity would disappear.

She didn't tell Beth the other thing that bothered her. The men were kind and caring and way too gentle. The bigger she got, the hornier she was.

And she was getting humongous.

Bigger and Bigger and Better

When she only had a few days left, Carrie Ann wondered if she were perhaps carrying twins. Her stomach was immense. The ultrasounds did not indicate any evidence of twins.

The day before Carrie Ann gave birth, the three men showed up together. Harold had been talking to her earlier that day and asked if he could come to see her.

Of course, she didn't know it was the day before. She did not have a date chosen for the baby's birth and while she knew what the purported due date was, she also knew that due dates were notorious for being missed.

Carrie Ann was horny and her horniness never stopped once during her pregnancy. However, all three men were too solicitous of her these past few weeks. Harold did have intercourse with her but he was gentle and steadfastly resisted pounding into her the way that she wanted him to.

When the three men showed up this night, her first thought was that they would be willing to relive the passion of their first encounter.

They had come close over the past couple of months. Carrie Ann did wonder how she could handle living without the constant petting and patting and caresses and nipple sucking and prodding with their huge cocks once the baby was born.

The men had brought food and non-alcoholic wine to celebrate the evening. They all knew her time was almost here.

Indeed, this was the purpose of the evening, Harold explained. "We have jointly decided that one of us will be with you until your time comes."

"What?" she said. "You cannot decide that."

"Well of course, with your permission, we decided this," Ben said.

"Yes, we don't want you to be alone," George said. "We care about you."

She scolded them for babying her and they laughed at her for saying "babying" and then she scolded them for being so gentle in bed.

Carrie Ann finally agreed that they could take care of her until her time was ready. "But there is something that you have to do for me."

"Anything," was the answer that all three gave.

"You have to give me a thorough fucking. I mean, a real good pounding. I need to feel like I am being drilled through the center with a big hard dick."

Harold started to protest. His cock twitched with the thought of driving itself all the way into Carrie Ann's snatch.

In his entire life, he had never had sex with a woman this far along and he thought that it should be a dream come true. But over the past few weeks, he realized that he had genuine feelings for her that went beyond sex.

It began with sex and he wondered if it would end with sex. But that was something to think about some other time. At the moment he was thinking about sucking on her tits and he wondered when her milk would start coming in.

That could be any day now. As he thought this, he reached behind her and unsnapped her bra. George and Ben decided that they would leave Harold alone with Carrie Ann and prepare a meal for all four of them.

While George and Ben cooked, Harold sucked and licked and caressed Carrie Ann's body. He nibbled on her clit and played with her slit, spreading her pussy lips wide and licking her.

He held her belly in his arms while he leaned over her and nuzzled his face in her breasts. She was squirming under him, moaning in pleasure.

He placed a pillow under her hips and kneeling between her legs, placed his cock against her pussy. It was hot and wet and eager, as always.

He used all his power to hold back his climax as he thrust into her from every angle he could manage. Her belly was huge and he watched her skin ripple as the baby repositioned itself.

That did it, watching the growing life inside Carrie Ann while he fucked her. He exploded in her.

Then he moved to lie beside her holding her in his arms. "Do you want some more?" He asked. She nodded.

Then she admitted that she was hungry. The smells of the meal that George and Ben were cooking wafted into the bedroom.

The four fuck buddies shared the meal and then they massaged Carrie Ann's entire body. Each man had a different part of her to pleasure. Back and neck. Each leg and foot.

They shared her belly, rubbing oils into her skin, gently kneading her flesh. Harold eventually went to the living room and stretched out on the sofa. Ben settled into the small single bed in the spare room.

George stayed with Carrie Ann, slowly stroking her body. He liked having her all to himself. He could revel in her body with all its hidden treasures.

She slept and he kept stroking her. Having her breasts there to use as he pleased, seeing her gigantic swollen tummy, knowing that he could have her any moment gave him a peaceful feeling of sensuality the like of which he had rarely felt before.

This night, Carrie Ann had a special glow about her. He could feel it radiating from her. She was drowsy and relaxed from the massage and stroking when he rolled her to her side, spooning her from behind as he wedged his cock between her legs and pushed it upwards until he found the wet hole.

She tilted her hips back toward him and allowed him to push deeper into her as he slowly fucked her from behind, his cock deep into her honey pot.

After he came inside her, they both slept. When George woke a couple of hours later, he needed to pee. He slowly moved out of the bed to pee, choosing to use the other bathroom rather than wake her by using the powder room.

When he emerged from the main bathroom, he encountered Ben. Ben was naked and his dick was rigid. "You going to pee with that?" George said.

George thought it was a stupid thing to say but what did you say to a naked man in the middle of the night. Ben looked at him sleepily, "I can think of something else I'd rather do with it."

George realized that he was being selfish in keeping Carrie Ann to himself so he suggested that Ben join him in Carrie Ann's bed.

The good thing about three men, Carrie Ann thought as she turned in the bed, in that lovely state between waking and sleeping, is that she never had to worry about them wearing out before she did.

When she thought back to sex in her pre-pregnancy days, she thought about the nights that she had drifted to sleep wanting more, even if she had fucked all evening.

Most men were satisfied a lot more easily than she was. She knew that if she wanted more right now, and she did, it was not far away. She smiled and let herself fall back into sleep.

Carrie Ann was sleeping on her back when Ben and George returned but she stirred awake as George got back into the bed. Ben was standing at the side of the bed, waiting for George to settle in.

Carrie Ann looked up at Ben and saw his cock standing at attention.

She reached for it and tugged him closer.

"Come here lover boy," Carrie Ann said, "I want some more of this."

Ben was all too willing to accommodate her desires.

Curvy Girls Do It On Dairy Farm

Irene

One of Amy's best friends since childhood came to visit Amy. She slept on the sofa in the living room and was happy to have a break from her life back home in the big city.

Maybe you know Amy? She's one of the original Curvy Girls. Her roommate Amanda is another one of the Curvy Girls.

They're busy little creatures sharing an apartment and studying hard in their respective graduate school fields. The third Curvy Girl is Beth who is already out in the working world.

These are three clever ladies who learned that the best way to have a fulfilling life is to find an efficient way to mix business with pleasure.

They have a roster of dates, a stable of studs, a bevy of bodacious boys who party with them, when they are in a party mode.

Usually the parties are held at Beth's house because it is big and spacious and has enough bedrooms for them to each have a private frolic but big enough beds to have a great big old skinfest if they are so inclined.

If Beth is too occupied to party, she either lets Amy and Amanda party at her place or the two of them opt to party in their apartment.

Their apartment is big enough, that is for sure. But it does not have the expensive décor that Beth has. From time to time, they all discuss sharing Beth's house.

They're all very busy women and about the only time all three of them would be together, it would be party time anyway.

But Amy and Amanda are in a stage of their lives where they don't know what will happen next. They both might head to another city to pursue graduate studies or one of them will.

Besides they have a lease for another year. And moving takes time and energy. They are all big proponents of "if it ain't broke, don't fix it."

Having Amy's best friend Irene sobbing on their sofa is causing some concern for both Amy and Amanda. Amy feels guilty because she doesn't have the time or inclination to listen to Irene's long repetitive tales about her ex-boyfriend.

Her boyfriend was really her fiancé but he ended the relationship and broke Irene's heart. Irene refused to say his name out loud. She was completely devastated and had even left her job.

She had to, she insisted, because that is where she met her fiancé and that is where he still works. She corrected herself and said, ex-fiancé.

Amy is also feeling guilty because she knows that having Irene there is cramping Amanda's life. Amanda likes to sit in the living room and read fiction as a part of her downtime relaxation.

How can a person relax with a big sobbing sniveler hogging the sofa and blowing her nose? Amanda says she doesn't care.

"You know, Amy," Amanda said, "Irene just needs to get laid. That would get her out of her mood." They were walking home from a seminar and Amy was apologizing for her friend taking up the living room.

Amanda waved away her friend's apology and continued, "It's hard to believe that she put so much energy into a man that she is wasting so much time crying over it."

Amanda also thought it was strange that Irene didn't have a job or some other thing in her life, besides the idiot fiancé, to focus on.

Amanda is an intense person who loves her chosen field so much, she sometimes regrets having to sleep. When she really needs a break, she knows what to do – have great sex and a lot of it.

That evening, Amanda talked to Irene about how important it was to get out there and have fun and find her passion in life.

Amanda looked at Irene and taking her reddened eyes into consideration and the puffy face and matted hair, she saw a very pretty woman.

While Amy, Amanda and Beth called themselves the Curvy Girls because they were slightly bent, Irene would qualify as a curvy girl because she was, well, very curvy.

Her breasts were enormous and her hips flared roundly out from her tiny waist.

What a shame to let a body like that not be out there having fun.

"You need to get laid," Amanda said.

Irene's response was a burst of fresh tears. "I can't. Oh, I can't. I just want to die."

Amanda shook her head in dismay. This is no way for a woman to live. She would have to find a solution. One of their fuckfests would not do the trick. Amanda was sure of that. Irene was a little too skittish for a group of horny people just having fun.

To The Farm

Amanda and Amy came up with the perfect solution. There was a dairy farm outside of the town where the university had experimental crops. One of their colleagues in another department had told them about it once upon a time.

The experimental part of the farm was an innovative addition that the university's clever administration came up with when it needed to expand the agricultural and ecological departments.

It was not financially feasible to set up an entire working farm, so they made a deal with a local farmer who had a huge farm. It's a tough time for farmers and the man was willing, more than willing, to lease out some of his acreage to the university and sell most of his dairy herd to the university as well.

The farmer only had one son who was in the business with him and the farmer's son was happy to participate in this endeavor if and when his father retired.

Amy had met the son. She had even considered asking him to join their play dates at Beth's but the son, whose name is Jason, seemed to be too occupied with his rural life to be available for raunchy nights with the busy ladies known as the Curvy Girls.

"So why didn't you ask him?" Amanda asked. "Is there something wrong with him?"

Amy shook her head. "No. I don't think there is anything wrong with him." She was pensive. It was hard to explain about Jason. He was a kind and gentle person but he was very serious.

Amanda and Amy went to visit Beth. It had been a busy time for them and they had not had the time for a good party for a while. They had to set up a play date anyway.

The plan that Beth came up with was nothing short of brilliant. They also planned a date night for

Saturday but that was for the three of them and whatever men showed up.

The Irene plan (as they called it) was to talk to Jason and have him meet Irene. They agreed they would tell Jason that their friend was just getting over grief and needed a day in the country and asked if he would mind letting her spend a few hours with him, observing how a farm works.

Farm Boy

Jason was forking hay into the cattle stalls. He loved farming and with the university deal in place, a lot of the stress was over and done. Completely gone.

And so was his father. Gone on a vacation with his wife, Jason's mother. The way his father relaxed now that the finances were so much better and the physical labor so much less, it was like he was a new man.

His father hinted that he and Jason's mother might make a permanent move to a warmer climate. This trip was a way for them all to decide if they liked not being on the farm and if Jason could handle it on his own.

Jason smiled at the notion that he could not handle the day to day operation by himself. He could and he even had spare time.

The only problem way that he had nothing to do with that time. It was ironic that he and his father (and mother) had struggled for years to get all the work done but now that he was on his own he could get it all done and have time left over.

Jason is twenty-six and while not a virgin by any means, he has not been laid in months. He thought that once the farm work leveled off, he would have more time to have fun with the ladies.

The university had been involved for a couple of years but it was only this summer that he and his father were really feeling the effects of the lightened work load because they had simply turned the big jobs over to the scientists.

The girls he used to chase were all gone off to their lives. Some were married, some were gone to the big city to chase careers.

There were not too many women left in the area and a farm boy just does not ride into town and charm the pants off the women there.

Besides they weren't his type. He wanted a big-boobed country girl who loved to fuck and suck any time of the day or night.

His cell phone rang at that moment, snapping him out of his reverie. It was a good thing, too, because his prick had leapt into action.

He was contemplating taking it out and running off a batch by hand right there in the barn. The smell of the baled hay was like sweet perfume to him. And that's when the phone rang.

He sighed and answered it.

Amy. He was surprised to hear from her. She was a cute little thing and she had hinted at getting together, just for fun but that was one of those frantic days in town and he didn't have the time or inclination to flirt back.

They had exchanged numbers anyway and here she was calling him.

He was surprised at her request but he liked it.

What she wanted was for him to have one of her friends spend a day with him. This Irene apparently was at some sort of crossroads in her life and Amy wanted to know if she could do a kind of "day at work" experience with him.

Why not?

It might be nice to have something different to do for a day, he thought.

A Setup for Passion

So Thursday afternoon, Irene headed out in a rented car and the GPS coordinates for the farm. It was about an hour drive from the town. Amy told her that it was a report that needed to be done but they didn't have time to drive out and get the information.

Irene didn't really understand the kind of research Amy was doing but she did agree with Amanda that this adventure would give Irene a chance to think about something other than her rotten ex-fiancé.

So when she pulled up to the farm, she was immediately charmed by the white house with the red trim on the shutters and all the out buildings that matched with their red roofs and doors.

She could see colorful fields reaching out around her as far as her eyes could see. A field on the left of the long lane held about a dozen black and white cows. The yard in front of the barn, also white with red trim, held a pickup truck, a tractor and a few other pieces of farm equipment that puzzled Irene.

She saw the man walking across the lawn in front of the house and for a moment, she was startled by her sudden realization that she did not want to be here.

She felt vulnerable and somewhat scared. The man was handsome, his checked blue shirt open down the front, his bronzed chest showing his muscles. He had a six-pack stomach, the like of which she had never seen before.

He was powerful and – hot. Really hot. The sudden burst of shy fear that she felt seemed to jar something loose in her.

When she stepped out of the car, she wanted to ask if she should leave her car where it was but no words came. Her mouth was dry and she could not get her eyes off his chest and stomach muscles.

A Roll in the Hay

As Jason shook her hand, Irene's voice returned. "The car is fine right where it is," he said.

Then he offered to give her a tour of the place. Amy insisted that Irene not take formal notes but just act as if it were just a visit to the farm. This would, Amy explained, make the report about impressions and that would be more powerful than a dry report of the height of the grain or whatever it was that could be measured.

Jason gave her a guided tour around the farm. He offered to take her to the fields but there were hundreds of acres of fields.

"It would be better if we could go on the four-wheeler," he said.

Irene agreed before she saw the four-wheeler. It looked like some sort of motorcycle hybrid. She had to hoist herself up on the seat behind him, with her legs spread in a very unladylike manner.

She had to hang onto him tightly as they bounced and jounced over the farm lanes from field to field. It took more than an hour to visit all the crops.

Jason wondered why Amy had asked specifically that he take Irene out on the four-wheeler. She seemed nervous to the point of jittery. If he hadn't enjoyed her enormous breasts pressed against his back so much, he might have suggested that they stop after she saw two or three fields.

He could feel the heat of her crotch through his jeans as it was pressed up against him. His cock was throbbing and he was so hard he wondered if his cock skin would split.

By the time they got back to the farm, Jason had to help Irene get down from the four-wheeler. She shook her body as if to get everything back in place.

He offered her coffee and she said all she wanted was water. She had moved to a stack of bales of hay that were near the cattle barn.

As she said she wanted water, she sat down. Jason had been going to ask her if she wanted to come into the house but he sensed that she was still a little joggled from the rough riding all terrain vehicle.

He had felt the way she clung to him on the bumpy parts and truth be told, he had gone out of his way to hit as many of the big bumps he could find.

"You just stay there," he said. "I'll be right back." After he left, heading for the house, Irene stood up and wandered to the barn door.

She could smell the animal smell from inside and gingerly stepped inside. There was a stack of hay bales off to her left. She was looking at the stalls in front of her and she wondered where the cows were.

She could smell them but there didn't seem to be any creature inside the barn at all.

"Oh there you are."

The voice startled Irene and she jumped.

"Oh," she said. Jason had a tray with a jug of water with ice and two tall glasses. He set it down on one of the bales of hay and moved two more down to serve as seats.

His shirt was still unbuttoned and Irene had a brief guilty pang. She had not once thought about her fiancé since she arrived on the farm.

The exhilaration of just being in the great outdoors was outstanding. And suddenly Irene felt herself laughing at something Jason said.

She knew how Amy and Amanda dealt with their personal sexual needs and as she looked at this handsome and powerfully built man, she could not help feeling a sense of freedom and attraction.

She owed no loyalty to anyone. Amy and Amanda told her to treat this like a holiday in the country. They didn't want her to think of it as work.

She was thinking these things when Jason leaned over and kissed her.

His lips were soft yet firm and she opened her mouth and his tongue was hot when it probed her mouth. She gasped and he whispered, "Do you mind?"

She shook her head, "I need this." Then she wondered what had come over her but she began to unbutton her own clothes.

He helped her.

Irene had heard the phrase, "a roll in the hay" but she never really thought about it until now. Hay was scratchy. She was stretched out over a couple of bales that somehow were pulled together.

Jason was leaning over her, kissing her, and fondling her breasts. She was used to the attention men paid to her breasts but this was different. Jason and kneading them with both of his hands in a more demanding way.

Her fiancé used to nibble and nip at her tits. He would suck her nipples pulling them into rigid, tight knots. He was rough with her boobs, squeezing them just a little too hard from time to time.

She loved having her breasts manhandled. She had told him this once and ever since, he had just kept on squeezing and pushing them together and often leaving bruises,

For the most part it was exciting but she could never really relax. Jason was firmly kneading her titties, one in each large hand but she soon realized that he was not going to surprise her painfully with a pinch or a squeeze that just was too hard.

She felt him move to her belly, pressing his hot hard cock against her softness and she was afraid she was going to orgasm then and there, the scratchy hay digging into her back.

He lifted her gently, his mouth back on hers and laid her on the floor, where their clothes lay scattered around.

Jason looked down at her as he arranged her on the floor. It was like a dream to have his prick pulsating against the white flesh of her gently rounded stomach as he lifted her from the hay to the clothes.

Her breasts were natural. He had always liked big breasts and had felt his share of them over the years.

He had seen ones just as big as Irene's but never any that were bigger. They were round, almost perfectly round with a slight sag at the bottom.

Of course, they were natural and as such they could not defy gravity. Her nipples were small and pebble-hard but they poked up as if they were reaching for him.

Her ass was plump and shapely and when he slid his hand between her smooth thighs, he could feel her heat amid her juices.

"I want you," he said, his words not much more than a groan. The floor was hard, too hard for her softness. He reached for an overall that had been freshly laundered and spread it over the bales of hay he had shoved together.

Then he lifted her up again and laid her down on the overalls. He knelt between her legs and spread her thighs, burying his face in her pussy lips.

She was sweet, like honey, and he drank deeply of her. She smelled like a flower, with some sweet spicy scent, pushing against his nose.

He found her clit with his tongue and he sucked on it, gently, feeling it unfold between his lips. He felt her round buttocks tense in his hands and he lifted them to him.

He had to have her. He wanted this more than he had ever wanted sex in his entire life. He rose up, moving his face up over her belly until he could bury it between her tits.

His cock was nestled against her, the head of it touching her pussy. One thrust and he would be part of her, inside her, her slick wetness wrapping itself around her.

If he didn't shoot his load all over her before he took that stroke.

Then, before he could do anything, she press herself against him, pushing her open cunt so that it absorbed the head of his cock and he had no choice but to push deeper into her.

She was short enough to fit perfectly in the cage of his thighs and arms but tall enough so that he could wallow in her tits while he fucked her, rocking her hard against the hay.

A Squirt in the Face

They were still naked on the bales of hay when Irene asked about the cows that she saw in the field. She wanted to know why the cows were outside when there was all the space inside.

Jason smiled. City girls were something else. This was why he didn't like dating them. They barely knew a cow from a goat.

He explained that the farm was a dairy farm. As well as the crops, there was a large herd of cattle in the large field that had once upon a time been his grandfathers.

The university was studying scientific ways to make the cows healthier and happier and more productive. The cows out front were the personal herd of Jason and his parents.

These cows provided their milk and other dairy products and shortly he would have to bring them in and milk them.

Irene was fascinated and began to ask if she could stay and watch. She looked somewhat like a cat licking the cream from her whiskers and Jason said, "Even better. I'll let you milk one."

This is how Irene ended up sitting on a three legged milking stool. She had watched, still naked except for her sandals, while Jason locked the braces around the necks of the cattle who dutifully strolled into the stalls and began to munch on the hay he had placed in the troughs at the front of the stalls.

He dug out this little stool, and showed her how to take the cow's teat in her hands and run her fingers firmly down the length of the teat.

"Make your hands suck the teat," he said. And as he demonstrated, instead of aiming the stream of milk into the pail that he set under the cow's udder, he streamed the milk towards Irene's boobs.

The milk was warm and Irene realized that should not be a surprise to her. Just because she bought milk from the cooler in the grocery store and kept it in the fridge at home, that did not mean that milk began as something cold.

Jason then squeezed a few more streams of cow's milk into the bucket. Irene began to work her fingers smoothly along the cow's teats and managed a couple of tiny dribbles. As she continued, Jason went to the other cows and attached milking machines to each of them.

Jason was wearing only boots as he did this. When he came back to Irene, she asked, "If you have those machines why did you get me to milk this cow."

"I thought you'd like the finger exercises."

Irene had picked up the rhythm that was needed and she aimed the next squirt of milk directly at his cock which was at half mast and rising.

She got a direct hit, right on the head, with the stream of milk.

"Now you'll have to lick it off," he said.

She turned so that her mouth was directly in front of his dick and she did lick the head of it. The milk tasted warm and sweet.

"I can't do any more right now," she said. "I have this cow to milk."

Jason squatted down beside her and took two teats in his hands and deftly milked the cow. Irene slid off the stool and stepped away so that he could finish the job.

Grass

Irene texted Amy to say that she would be late coming back to the apartment.

Amy texted her back and said, "Take your time."

She watched Jason deal with the milk and unlock the cows so they could roam back outside again.

It was dinner time and Jason asked her if she would stay and have dinner with him. It would be nothing special, he said.

Irene followed him into the house, each of them carrying their clothes. She had thought perhaps he would want to pick up on the dick licking in the barn but after he freed the cows, he suggested dinner.

They were in the house and he was doing something with the oven and his back was to her. She liked his ass. It was high and firm.

And that was the first time she thought of her fiancé all afternoon. His ass was flat, like some sort of last minute addition that was slapped on to connect his legs to his body.

Irene grinned. She hardly ever thought negative thoughts about the man who broke her heart, even after he broke her heart.

Jason caught her grinning and asked her something but she had not been listening and all she heard was "grass." She thought he asked her if she wanted some grass.

She looked at him, trying to sort out his words while she came back to the moment. She was not used to calling marijuana "grass" but this was a different world, out here on the dairy farm.

She nodded.

He took her hand and led her through the patio doors that opened off the kitchen to a small garden area and he folded himself down on the grass.

She laughed as she sat beside him. He looked at her quizzically and she said, "I thought you asked if I wanted to smoke grass."

He laughed too. "Afraid not. I just asked if you wanted to sit out here on the grass while dinner finished cooking."

He reached for her breasts and leaning forward, kissed each of them. They both smelled slightly of the barn and of sex.

Irene wondered if she had lost her mind. She had slept with a couple of boyfriends before she met her fiancé. Ex-fiancé. But she had never been casual about sex.

But here she was, naked in some area she didn't even know the name of, with a man whose last name she didn't know.

And she was with cow teat smell on her hands, sitting bare-assed on the grass, letting this strange man feel her up.

And she was horny.

She wanted to fall to her back and spread her legs and have him fuck her hard and long, grasping her ass and pulling her up to meet his pounding cock.

She reached for his cock, which was back to its full hardness.

She took the head first, using her lips to squeeze it tight while she wiggled her tongue around it. Then she opened her mouth wider and slid his cock as far into her mouth as she could.

She could feel the veins and the pulsing and it turned her on. She tasted his precum. She even tasted her own taste. Neither of them had washed or showered since the episode on the hay bales.

Unbidden, the fiancé popped into her mind again. Him with his fastidious scrubbing and scouring before and after.

With wild abandon, Irene moved her mouth from Jason's cock to his balls.

They were pulled up tight in their sac and she licked the tight dark skin that held his balls. He moaned and Irene liked that. She felt in control.

She could do anything she wanted to do and she knew that without saying a word or hearing a word. She could explore this man's entire body and he would let her do it.

Once she had tried this very thing, licking his balls, and her fiancé had grabbed her hair and asked where she had learned this trick. Not only did this ruin the moment, it caused a fight that lasted for a week.

Jason didn't care. He was just having fun, like she was.

Irene played with the stem of his cock, the part that runs under his balls, stroking it with long firm strokes that passed between his balls.

Then she did something she had never done before. She guided Jason to lie on his back and lowered her tender snatch over his rigid pole.

It made her gasp. She could feel the end of his cock pressing against something inside her and she bounced a couple of times, lightly.

This let her get used to the full feeling of hard cock before she began pumping herself on him in earnest. He was very broad chested and she did not have to worry about hurting him, like she did with her fiancé. She leaned forward, still pumping her hips vigorously, so he could suck her hard nipples and play with her full breasts.

When her climax came, it came in waves, each wave more intense. She wanted to stop before she fainted but she did not want to stop because each stroke was exquisite.

He nibbled and sucked and squeezed her enormous tits until she collapsed in a heap on top of him. She was vaguely aware that he did not come again and was trying to say something to him about taking care of him as soon as she caught her breath.

He was still hard inside her and he stayed like that while he rolled her to her back, wrapping her ankles around his shoulders.

He was kneeling, his hands holding her round ass in his big hands, and he began slowly sliding his prick in and out, in and out.

His pace quickened and Irene felt a tingle of an orgasmic aftershock when she realized that he was about to dump an enormous load in her.

Cherry Orchard

After dinner which barely missed being scorched in the oven while they were outside on the grass, Jason invited Irene to stay the night.

He even offered her one of the spare rooms. He genuinely didn't want her driving home in the dark in an area that she did not know well.

She texted Amy again and said she would be back the following day. She also set herself up in a spare room but she didn't spend more than five minutes in it.

She showered and still wrapped in a towel, she strolled into Jason's room. He was sitting in bed, propped up on a pile of pillows, his arms behind his head.

Irene went and settled into the bed beside him, resting her head on his chest. She dozed off in this position and woke sometime in the middle of the night, spooned up with her back against his chest, his cock back to life and nudging against her ass.

She shifted so that she could feel the heat of his cock head slip between her buttocks. She pushed back against him and suddenly she was on fire again. Her tits tingled for his attention and then his arms were around her and his hands were firmly clamped over her breasts.

Irene arched her back and for the third time, Jason fucked her into an earth-shaking climax. Irene's body was in ecstasy and her mind was free-floating.

She had never known such abandonment in her life. There were no rules here on the farm. Jason's body was a natural treat, deeply muscled from the farm work. She was used to men like her fiancé with their gym-inspired abs and biceps.

Jason had muscles upon muscles, smoothly formed and molded into a shape that she had only seen in fine art sculptures.

She felt safe and secure in his embrace and best of all, there were no stipulations. If she came four times before he let himself explode, he reveled in her joyous screams.

He withdrew his cock and went down on her, sucking eagerly and her pussy was damp with her own juices. He burrowed his face into her and then looked up at her, licking his lips.

"You are one tasty woman," he said and went back down to suck and lick some more. Irene could not prevent herself from comparing this to her ex-fiancé who would not go down on her at all.

He was too concerned about cleanliness. Not just the cleanliness of her cunt, but the cleanliness of the sheets on the bed. They had to use a soft towel under them and she knew that he adjusted his passion so they didn't stray off the towel and get semen stains or pussy juice on the sheets.

Irene banished thoughts of her ex-fiancé from her mind and turned her attention to the man in bed with her.

When he got up to milk the cows, she offered to go with him but he said that he wanted to get it done and not be distracted by her.

"That way, I can get back here faster," he said, and he did. It was less than an hour when he came back to bed and they played and snoozed until mid morning.

For Jason, this was a turning point in his life. He knew that he could live the rural life he wanted and find pleasure without having to travel out of his element. As he stretched, his body was completely relaxed.

Jason knew that it was a lot easier to think about life when his entire being was not focused on relieving the urgent and burning desire to plow his cock into a warm, wet and willing hole.

Irene was shocked when she showered and dressed and drank her coffee at how the whole door to her previous life had closed so firmly. Two days ago she was sobbing over her lost love.

She was beginning to understand now that her grief was not for the marriage that never would take place.

It was not even grief. It was fear. Fear of the unknown.

Jason and Irene were sitting on a bench in the cherry orchard. The cherries were past the blossom stage but they were not fully developed as edible fruit. They were beautiful and with the sun dappling the area around the trees and Irene and Jason, Irene understood that life was all about living in the moment.

She didn't know what the future held but it no longer scared her. She smiled at Jason over the top of her coffee mug. She saw the symbolism in the unformed cherries that hung over her head.

She was like these hard little unripe fruit but she knew she was firmly attached to the earth again and that in due time she would ripen into a life that was perfect for her.

Who knew, maybe she would come back here again. Jason's body was indeed a work of art. Her body was fulfilled like it had never been fulfilled in its entire life.

She had to drive back to Amy's to start considering what she might do next. Whatever it was, it was all up to her.

Curvy Girls Do It Naughty

Urge to Kill

Kate was in a rage. This wasn't the first time it happened and she could be sure it wasn't the last time it would happen.

If she were writing a play, she would label this, "Scene with husband and really boring sex."

For Kate it was really complicated. She lay in bed, a cotton sheet covering her from the waist down. Gerard was already on his side, his back to her, snoring.

Kate stared at the ceiling and contemplated doing herself. Her favorite way to masturbate involved a pair of wooden clothes pins and her multispeed vibrator. She pinched her nipples as she imagined clamping the clothes pins on them.

She reached down between her legs and found her little knob. Rolling it between her thumb and forefinger she could feel the shape of it. It was like a little tiny penis with the shaft and the swollen head.

It was maybe a quarter inch long but she was sure that there were just as many nerve endings in her clit head as there were in Gerard's entire cock.

She could feel Gerard's semen trickling out of her cunt. At least it made good lubricant. She dipped her fingers inside and got them nice and damp.

She played with her clitoris, stroking it and lubricating it, with one hand while the other hand pinched her nipples. She did manage to achieve an orgasm but it was really small and really weak.

It wasn't more than a little shiver that ran along the length of her clit and up to her navel. It wasn't what she craved but it was better than nothing. It certainly was better than what Gerard had offered up in the way of wild sex.

Kate tried to get to sleep and eventually she succeeded, promising herself a proper session with her vibrator in the morning. Gerard had to go to work an hour before she did and that would give her the golden opportunity to attend to her horny needs.

She looked at him sleeping, his back to her and his bare butt pointed in her direction. It was really frustrating to look at him and know that he has the equipment and the body to show her the time of her life.

But he wouldn't or he couldn't. Whatever it was, it was destroying Kate. She used to think there was no such thing as bad sex. She was wrong.

Sex with Gerard was a never ending series of almost there but never arriving. Kate began to cry without even realizing that her tears were so close to the surface. Her puny self-induced orgasm was not enough to sustain her for the rest of her life, even if she did it to herself three times a day.

Lately, Kate had begun to think how convenient it would be if Gerard just died. This unbidden thought was so horrendous to her that she felt immediately guilty even though she had not consciously conjured thought.

She really didn't want Gerard dead. She just wanted him out of her life. As she lay there hand still resting on her crotch, Kate decided to follow her line of thinking just to see where it took her.

It took her to the core of her being. She needed good sex, good lovemaking, good fun. She wanted to get down and dirty, to revel in the sheer naughtiness of sex.

Kate was 30 years old. She worked hard at keeping her body taut and toned. Her legs were long and slender with delicate ankles. Her ass was high and smooth. Her waist was neat and trim and her breasts were full yet perky.

At least once a week, Gerard made love to her. Or at least that was how he thought of it. Making love. This is how that worked.

They would go to bed, he would kiss her lightly on the cheek, while sniffing to see if she had just got out of the shower. He didn't know that she knew that's what he did but that is what he did.

Then like some sort of preprogrammed robot, he began. He licked her neck, paid equal attention to both breasts nibbling them dutifully, and move down to her pussy.

He licked his tongue up one side of her pussy, ran his tongue roughly over her clit and then licked down the other side. Then he would put two fingers inside her and wiggled them back and forth.

At this point, Kate skin felt like it was ready to snap and split. Then Gerard would get up on his knees and lean over her with his cock in his hand.

He would insert carefully into her pussy and then start a rhythmic in and out pushing and pulling, pushing and pulling, pushing and pulling.

Finally, with a great burst of energy he would slam his cock into her three times in a row and freeze solid holding himself in that position while he shot his load deep into her.

Kate felt like a piece of warm liver and she hated that feeling. It didn't help to know that she was complicit in this routine. If she felt that she could talk to Gerard, that would be one thing but she didn't feel that she could talk to him.

Outside the bedroom, she and Gerard had so much in common. They had the same life goals, the same taste in music and decor, and they both liked the same friends. It's just that Kate could not stand the lack of fulfillment in her marriage bed.

If she went to a marriage counselor, the counselor would not understand. All Kate had to do was talk to Gerard. But that was impossible.

The irony was that while Kate could not imagine shaking Gerard up in bed, she could picture him dead. Right now she was angry enough to kill him.

By the time she got to work, Kate realized that she was losing her mind she was losing all common sense, she was losing her judgment, and if she didn't do something soon she would lose the entire life she had planned out in front of her.

To Hell with You

Kate was in the lunchroom at work, smiling at her colleagues as they came in and picked up their lunch. Some ate at the desk, some ate outside because it was sunny. Kate sat alone. She wasn't close to any of her coworkers.

She had a couple of friends in the office but they weren't the kind of friends that you share the innermost secrets of your life with. One of her better friends at work was Beth.

Beth was elegant and slender and vibrant in a pale blonde sort of way. Beth came into the lunchroom and got her lunch of the fridge. She smiled at Kate and sat down across from her.

As she looked at Kate, Beth's smile faded. "Are you all right," Beth asked..

Kate nodded.

Beth reached out and laid a hand over Kate's. "You know you can always talk to me. I'm a pretty good listener."

Kate smiled at her and waved a hand. "It's just one of those married life things." Immediately Kate regretted saying it like this. She knew Beth was single and she didn't want to sound arrogant.

Some people who were single could take what she said as if she were shutting them out, putting herself on a pedestal because she had a husband and the other person didn't.

Assume she started thinking these thoughts, Kate knew that she was in trouble. She was thinking like a silly teenage girl. It was on becoming to her and it was rude to Beth.

In an effort to overcome her awkwardness, Kate said. "Maybe it's what they call the seven-year itch except that it's only been three years."

Beth smiled at her in a very knowing way. "Let's go for a drink after work," Beth said. "Sometimes a little girl talk can solve a lot of problems."

Beth was in the bar next to the office a few minutes before Kate. She liked Kate. Kate was good at her job and a very pleasant person. Lately Beth noticed that Kate was not her usual self.

Beth half expected Kate not to show up but she did. Kate slipped into the chair across from Beth and they ordered glasses of white wine.

It didn't take long for Kate to start talking and they had not even finished the first glass of wine, Kate had barely taken a sip out of hers, when Kate blurted out, "I just want to scream at Gerard to hell with you. And I don't know why."

"Don't you?" Beth said

What's a Woman Supposed to Do?

Kate told Beth her story. Everything was perfect, she explained, except for the sex. It could be a lot worse. Kate knew it could be a lot worse.

Gerard didn't run around on her. He didn't neglect her in bed... And this is where Beth held up a hand. "That depends on how you look at," Beth said.

"I call it neglect," Beth paused. She ordered another round of wine. "I'm a firm believer that every woman is responsible for her own satisfaction in bed. And I'm not talking about masturbation. I'm talking about getting the sex you want to making the guy love giving it to you."

"But," said Kate, "what's a woman supposed to do?" She looked down at her hands. She was not use to talking about sex, especially not with someone from work.

"She supposed to have fun."

What Kate didn't know about Beth, was that Beth was a very highly charged sexual person. There was a time when Beth thought that she could not get enough sex to ever satisfy her.

Not too long ago, Beth found the solution. She and a couple of her friends who were just as busy as Beth came up with the perfect plan. They were smart ladies and they knew that traditionally men and women had different sexual natures.

It was supposed to be some sort of biological imperative that kept the human race running smoothly. Men spread their seeds to as many women as they could screw while the women kept popping out babies.

Historically, this was a good thing. Beth had no desire to whatever get married and have children or even to stay single and have children.

She wanted to have fabulous sex when she wanted it and she wanted the man to understand that it was all about fun.

Beth was one of the original curvy girls. This is how she and her friends referred to themselves. It was a bit of an inside joke because they were not only referring to their bounteous curves but they were also referring to the slight bend in a sexual natures.

They were women of the 21st century with great expectations of their lovers. The guys had to be well hung, fun-loving, healthy and energetic. No narrow-minded men need apply.

Beth had an expert eye for frustrated women and she had known for some time that Kate was frustrated. She was not surprised. It often happened to people who got married and lost the ability to speak up for themselves in bed.

"You need to get laid," Beth said. "It is as simple as that." Before Kate could protest, Beth put up her hand. "I'm not talking about picking up some guy in a bar or doing someone at work. I'm talking about just getting laid and having fun doing it."

"But I'm married. I can't do that to Gerard."

Kate sipped her wine. "If I could talk to Gerard about sex therapy, this wouldn't be a problem. Because then that would mean I could talk to him about sex."

Beth looked at her and made an instant decision. Kate was just too tightly wrapped, too anal-retentive, to talk to her husband about something this important.

Beth's decision was to tell Kate about the curvy girls and how they handle their sexual needs. It was really quite simple.

To make it really efficient, the curvy girls tended to triple date. That is the three of them would contact one of the guys and suggest they all get together, usually at Beth's house.

Each guy knew the rules. No one got involved and if one of the guys moved on to a permanent relationship, no one's feelings were hurt.

"Think about it," Beth said. "Come over to my house for dinner and I'll invite one of my good fuck buddies for me and some handsome virile dude for you."

Then Beth had a thought. "If you cannot imagine yourself doing this, why don't you both come over and will have a nice quiet sedate evening where I fuck Gerard and one of these guys entertains you."

Kate stared at her work colleague, and her jaw dropped. The rush of excitement was so great, her panties were wet. She was just soaked in her own juices.

She thought how ridiculous she was to protest at Beth's suggestion when just last night she wished Gerard would die. She knew that the thought was one of those dreadful things that pops into your mind and that she would be devastated if she lost Gerard.

She also knew that something had to give or else she would snap someday and lose her temper and that could kill the marriage.

Doing the Dirty

On Friday, Kate called Gerard at work and told him that she planned to go to dinner with Beth. It was a work thing. It was unusual for Kate not to announce her plans several days in advance.

But she didn't dare mention this to Gerard, face to face at home. She knew that her nervousness would show. She had mentioned Beth numerous times in the past so it was no big surprise to say that she was going to have dinner with Beth.

She was at Beth's having a glass of wine when the men arrived. They had arrived separately and didn't seem to know each other too terribly well but they came at the same time.

They were relaxed and casual and the four of them sat in Beth's living room, chatting like old friends. There was no dinner. That was just a story for Gerard.

One of the men, a guy named Boyd, engaged Kate in a conversation about flower gardening. He was a biologist and very knowledgeable. He picked up her hand as they talked and began gently massaging her fingers.

She was shocked at how erotic it was to have him take each bone and joint of each hand and manipulate it in a slow massage. She was a devotee of manicures and always opted for the full hand massage but she had never felt anything like this.

Beth and her friend discreetly disappeared and let Kate enjoy Boyd's attention. Eventually, because she is Kate and therefore prone to worry, Kate asked, "have you been here before – at Beth's?"

He nodded, "yes."

He lifted her hand and kissed her palm. "Have you?"

Kate looked into his eyes and felt almost dizzy. There was something about the dimly lit room and the soft background music. She didn't even notice that Beth had turned down the lights and turned up the music but she did notice a mood that was very conducive to relaxation.

Boyd leaned over and kissed her throat, running his tongue along the front of her neck. He whispered, "You just let me know if you ever want me to stop."

Kate moaned in reply and her moan could've been a yes or it could've been a no. However the way she arched her back moving her throat closer to him was definitely a yes.

Boyd was longer boned and more slender than her husband but the muscles in his shoulders and arms were thick and shapely. He guided her into the bedroom that was just down the hall from the living room.

He lifted her to the bed and returned to her neck letting his lips moved to the point of her jaw bone just under her ear. Kate had her ears nibbled on before but never in this seductive way.

"Let go." He said, "Let it happen. Just let it happen."

When Boyd felt her body relax, even though it was not a full relaxation, he glided to her ankles and took each foot one at a time into his capable hands. He used reflexology techniques and Kate recognized this from her experience in having reflexology administered in the hopes that her persistent headaches could be relieved.

However she had never felt anything like this. By the time he began moving his mouth up to the back of her needs and down her inner thighs, Kate was putty in his hands. When he reached under her ass to pull her panties down over her hips, she lifted her hips to make it easier for him to remove the wisp of silk panties. When he buried his face in her neatly trimmed bush, Kate did not flinch.

Boyd sucked her juices and flicked her clit with his tongue. He licked down past her pussy to the delicate skin between her cunt and her anus.

It was a strange sensation for Kate to feel the ripple of nerve endings under her skin. Usually Kate struggled for control not just in bed but in all aspects of her life. Once, when she was in college, she had gone to hypnotist with friends of hers.

The hypnotist told her she was unusually difficult to hypnotize. Kate took this as a compliment and she considered herself hyper vigilant about everything in her life.

She read every line of her credit card statements and bank statements. She went over every grocery bill the minute she got home and put the groceries away.

When she was in bed with her husband, she always felt like she was watching the whole procedure as if she was sitting in a chair next to the bed and observing what he did and how she reacted.

It had been almost an hour from the time that Boyd began playing with her fingers and he finally reached the core of her sexual being. She wanted him to rise up and shove his penis inside her, she wanted to wrap her ankles around his neck.

She wanted him to take her. She was struggling to hold onto her control, he lifted up his head and kissed her lower belly. He moved his hands under her buttocks and used his fingers and thumbs as little individual massage elements.

He touched her body in places that she never remembered being touched before. His hands on her ass were not taking random tours of her flesh. His thumbs met in the little dimple just above the crack of her ass and he began moving them in circular motion.

This thumbs must be touching a pressure point because each gyration of the thumbs sent tingles all along her spine and up through the muscles of her neck into the back of her skull.

Then his magic fingers began moving up her spine one vertebra at a time as he moved up over her his body rose above her until his extremely thick and very hard cock was pressing against her belly where his mouth had just been.

His hands moved down and lifted her torso up so that her breasts were against his chest. In one gigantic swoop, Boyd rolled to his back and lifted her so that she was poised with her wet and eager cunt hovering directly over his cock.

She was drenched. She felt a gush of her own body fluids trickle down her inner thighs.

"Are you ready?" He asked.

"Yes."

Her voice was barely a whisper and then she felt it, the hot hard heat of his erection pressing into her with such force that she was sure he would be spreading her pelvic bones apart.

He held her with his hands on her waist and thrust himself slowly into her. She could feel the end of his cock somewhere inside her rearranging her internal organs.

Her clit brushed against the base of his penis, each thrust touching and breaking close to an orgasm that was already making her blood run alternately icy cold and steaming hot.

Each time she struggled to reach back into her center of control, he moved his hands his fingers still playing a tune on her bones and control slipped out of her grasp.

Without withdrawing from her body, Boyd rolled them over as if they were one beast so that he was poised between her legs still deep inside her. He lifted her ass up in position to himself so that each stroke rubbed harshly against her clitoris.

Then it happened.

The orgasm began and it felt like she was being split into two pieces. It was a release like peeing after suffering with a full bladder and gentle like big warm waves washing over her body and shuddering like being hit by a bolt of lightning.

Kate felt like she had blacked out and was just coming to, dizzy and confused. Still the orgasm continued as he slowly rode her swollen pussy into subsidiary orgasms like ripples after a big wave.

Fast Time Pastime

Boyd looked down at Kate's face and saw years literally drop away and she grimaced in a pain/pleasure combination of sensual experiences.

Boyd was a biologist but he had financed his college education with reflexology and neurolinguistic programming. These were techniques that he used successfully in relaxation coaching.

The two of them provided an intense one-two combination of mind and body control techniques. He had known Beth since their days at University and had used his magic fingers to relax Beth through reflexology.

Boyd was busily writing a book on finding the secret to relaxation success. He loved people but he loved them in the abstract.

When Beth called him to tell him about her friend Kate he was more than willing to help guide Kate into the finer things in life such as really good sex.

Boyd wasn't completely altruistic. He loved the intimacy of sex and the feeling of a woman tremble under his touch. He knew how to guide them into a state of relaxation that removed all mental obstacles from their cluttered minds.

He had always respected Beth and the first time he came to one of her house parties, he was enchanted by the concept of sex the sake of sex.

He thought of it as a Zen like mindfulness approach to sex. They were no mind games and no ulterior motives and no expectations other than the need of nothing but pleasure.

He referred to it in conversation with Beth as a fast time pastime. He didn't come often to Beth's because usually he was occupied with work, writing and some ongoing clients who needed minor adjustments in their psyche.

He could almost predict that within the next half hour Kate would begin to feel huge guilt pangs.

However he knew how to guide her past the worst of those pangs. They would talk and cuddle but not in an overtly sexual way.

He was torn between wanting to fuck her again and wanting to explode inside her. It was possible he could do both. It'd been more than a month since the last time he had enjoyed the pleasure of a woman's soft sweet flesh.

Kate was beautiful. Her body was a work of art. He could tell what she was capable of even bigger orgasms and if he had a chance to take her away for a weekend he could revel in teaching her so many techniques guaranteed to improve everything about her life.

He had been riding her slowly while she writhed and moaned under him, her fingers digging into his ass. He could feel his balls tighten and the urgency of his need to climax.

With three powerful thrusts he emptied himself pumping stream after stream of his semen into her. Afterwards he held her and they rested.

They had spent two hours in bed and he asked her if she had any time constraints.

Get Me Out of Here

Kate was surprised at her response. She was a woman who lived with the rigid time constraints. She always had time constraints. Sometimes even resented taking the time to pee.

Her first reaction in any social situation was "get me out of here." Even when she was on her way to Beth's earlier this evening she regretted making the appointment.

So when Boyd asked if she had any time constraints, she was surprised that her answer was "no." What surprised her even more was that she continued, "I don't think I even have any bones."

Then she laughed. For a brief instant she wondered if she had been drugged. She felt a sense of relaxation that surprised her. She was aware of Boyd and she was aware of the glowing feelings that streamed through her body and she didn't want to move.

She was encased in a bubble of incredible tranquility and she didn't want to even think about stepping out of that precious moment.

"Good." Boyd said. And he began again. This time he led Kate down a path into her inner naughtiness where he urged her to tell him the biggest sexual secret she held inside her head.

He didn't push her or try to convince her to speak but he simply acknowledged her refusal to tell him her deep dark secrets and kept on talking about things that he liked to do.

As he spoke, he turned her over and spread her smooth white cheeks and delicately probed her pink little anus with the tender tips of his fingers.

He licked the space between her anus and her wet pussy tasting his own seed. He felt her tense ever so slightly and he gradually slowed down the attention he was playing to tiny anal orifice.

He turned his attention to the soles of her feet, the back of her knees, her lower belly and her elbows. He spoke to her in a gentle and hypnotic voice. He wasn't hypnotizing her but he was guiding her into the deep recesses of her subconscious.

As he talked to her, admiring her body he guided her hands to his body. She took his ball sack in one hand and then both hands lifting his testicles gently cupping them one in each hand.

Her hands were soft but she held his balls firmly applying just enough pressure to bring pleasure that was on the right side of pain. It was pure pleasure and he felt himself becoming aroused again.

He guided her to her stomach and worked his way up the right leg and then the left leg touching every square inch of her skin between her ankles and her hips. Pleasure relaxed her and this time when he spread her cheeks began to play with her ass hole she lifted her hips to meet his eager tongue.

The skin around her nether opening was smooth and cool. He tongued her tiny opening. He moved up so that his cock was pressed between her cheeks. He knew that she would need more lubrication to accommodate his cock in her anal passage.

He knew that he want to go slow with her and bring her back to a peak of action without interrupting her easy acceptance of new sensations.

He knelt behind her lifting her hips up so that her wet snatch was at the end of his cock. She was on her knees with her head down on the bed in her hands bracing herself. He reached around her took her breasts in his hands as he slid his penis back into her.

Her orgasm began almost immediately. It was slower and longer than the previous one and as she was coming to a shuddering end, he unloaded into her for the second time that evening.

Can an Old Dog Learn New Tricks?

Kate barely remembered how she and Boyd moved from the bedroom to the living room. She knew they showered and she knew they were dressed but she was floating. It wasn't like being stoned and it wasn't like being drunk.

It was like being child again with the complete freedom not to have to worry about anything or think about anything other than the pleasure of movement.

Part of her wanted to go to sleep immediately and part of her wanted to bask in the sensations of the moment. She hugged Boyd and thanked him for a lovely evening. She shut her eyes and smiled. Such an understatement.

After Boyd left she went back into the living room where Beth was sitting, sipping her glass of wine. She didn't ask, she just poured Kate a similar glass of wine.

"Are you all right?" Beth asked with a big grin on her face.

"Oh yes," Kate replied. "I'm better than all right."

"Will you be all right to drive home?" Beth asked. "Perhaps I shouldn't have offered you that wine."

"Oh I'm all right. It's not the wine that's affecting me. I can call Gerard to come and pick me up if I need to."

Beth raised an eyebrow.

Kate realized how ridiculous that might sound to ask her husband to come and pick her up because she had just been fucked. She laughed.

"I was thinking that I might just tell him I've had too many glasses of wine and he can bring a cab over here."

Kate looked like she was floating. She looked up at Beth. "Really Beth, I'm fine."

Kate sipped her wine. "Then I realized if I got him out of the house to come and get me because I had too much to drink, it would alleviate that potentially awkward moment."

She paused. "And for some reason I think it would be good for Gerard to step out of his routine too."

Kate gaze into her wine glass and said softly, "If this old dog can learn new tricks so can that old dog."

Kate had a second glass of wine and then called Gerard. She didn't enter into a debate or discussion with him about the wisdom of him taking a cab over to Beth's and driving her home in her car.

She gave him Beth's address and hung up. Beth met Gerard at the front door and invited him in. She made espresso and three of them sat companionably in the living room discussing a book that Beth was reading and that was laying face down onto the table.

Kate was aware that Gerard was being very calm. After she hung up the phone she had a twinge of guilt. She had been very naughty but she was still mellow from her naughtiness.

She felt a sea change, something deep inside her had shifted. She had glimmers of feeling like this in the past but the glimmers always managed to slip away just beyond her grasp. They were usually the aftermath of a good night's sleep filled with dreams, good dreams.

When they got home, Gerard helped her into the house. She really wasn't that drunk, she was barely drunk at all but she wasn't ready for any serious discussion and she would never be ready for an explanation.

She said, "I really appreciate you coming to pick me up."

He said, "I really appreciate being asked."

Kate looked at him and she must've looked quizzical because he said, "You never ask me to do anything for you. It made me feel good that you needed me tonight."

For a brief moment Kate saw the man she married. She didn't want this moment to end. She wondered what the right words were to explain how she felt.

She couldn't exactly tell him that she thought of him all evening because she didn't. She didn't think at all.

She smiled at him flirtatiously. "Can I ask you something else?"

"Of course you can."

"Could you put me to bed? I think I'm going to fall asleep on my feet."

And he did. He helped her out of her clothes and into her nightie. The bedroom lights were dim and Kate felt dreamlike as he tucked her in.

She really didn't want to go to sleep because she was afraid she would wake up in the morning and this feeling would be gone.

Ah, she thought, she could arrange a repeat with Boyd until she could learn to reach this feeling all by herself. She wasn't exactly sure what had happened but it was more than sex.

When Kate woke in the morning, Gerard had brought in a train with her favorite Saturday morning newspaper and a perfect cup of coffee. This was one of the traditions in their household.

Gerard was propped up on his side of the bed reading the sports section. Kate was thrilled to realize the feeling was still with her.

She asked him, "What is the kinkiest thing you ever wanted to do in bed?"

He gave her half smile and said, "You first. What's your favorite kinky fantasy?"

She replied, "Not fair. I asked first."

Their eyes met and held each other's gaze. "I don't think ahead any kinky fantasies," he said.

"Well do you have any fantasies even if they are not kinky." She held up her hand and said, "You're not allowed to ask me the same question."

"Oh they're that kinky are they?" He grinned playfully at her and tossed his paper to the floor.

"I'd much rather show you than tell you," he said. He reached for her and she tossed her newspaper to the floor as well.

"Hello, complete stranger whom I never met before this morning," he said. "I want to do some very naughty things to you."

And thus began a mutual exploration into the hidden secrets that each of them, Gerard and Kate, had been hiding in the clandestine unshared spaces in their minds. They agreed, almost without words, to lose themselves in each other without analyzing what they did and why they did it.

They just did it. They licked and sucked and nibbled and bit, it took all weekend but they explored every square inch of each other's bodies. They kissed each other in places that they had never seen before. They did things that they had never done with each other before.

Kate knew that whatever this was, it had only just begun.

Curvy Girls Do It Married and Dirty

The Bored Housewife

One of Beth's oldest friends had a rare capacity in Beth's world. She made Beth feel a wave of envy that was so strong, it was like jealousy sometimes.

They competed in high school for marks and grades and awards and when they went to university, the competition continued. They were both cool, as in icy cool, blondes with an organized sense of being.

At University, they were winners. They got good grades, won awards, and they were even among the prettiest girls on campus.

Beth was driven by her need to make money and when they graduated, Beth stepped immediately into the corporate world where her success continued. She was really good at what she did and she never had to bring out the bitch side of her anymore.

Georgia was driven by her need to be free and independent and she opened up her own consulting business. Beth struggled with her torn desire to see her friend succeed – but not too much – and her mean little secret desire to see Georgia fail.

Georgia needed to have at least one failure in her life, Beth thought but she was ashamed of this tiny streak of meanness.

Georgia succeeded beyond her wildest expectations. And then to add insult to injury, Georgia met and married a hunk of a man. Beth was still single.

However the good news for Beth was that she liked being single.

She had a special friend and extracurricular activities that ensured her the most satisfying sex life any woman could imagine. Her time was her own and she was the master of her own universe.

Beth was always a little bit surprised that her little jealousy of Georgia's life appeared. She searched her soul but she could not figure out why she would feel this way. It didn't make sense to her.

Georgia's husband, Hank, was tall, dark and handsome. He had money and power and broad shoulders. To make matters even worse, Beth liked him.

Not in that sexual attraction like kind of way but in an admiring kind of way. Beth loved being single because she didn't like sharing her time or her life with someone all the time.

And at the moment, Beth was sitting alone at a tiny table in her favorite quaint little bistro, waiting for Georgia to show up. It was odd that even though they only lived an hour's drive from each other, it was rare that they got together.

They had emailed over the last couple of years but Georgia was in town with her precious husband for some special event.

Beth snarled inwardly, likely getting a Nobel Prize for something. Then she stopped herself. What was wrong with her?

She loved Georgia and this was a very unbecoming attitude. Beth was working through her angst over why only Georgia got her into this kind of mood. It was not just competitiveness.

Before Beth could dig into the reasons for her nastiness toward Georgia – even if it was a well-hidden and not conscious nastiness – the woman herself appeared.

She was not late. Beth had been there early. It gave her an advantage, she thought, to be the first person to arrive at any meeting, even if the meeting was with her best friend forever.

Beth needed an edge, all the time and everywhere. She had to be number one.

She smiled and rose to greet Georgia. They embraced and then smiled and complimented each other on how well they both looked. And it was not a lie from either of them.

Beth and Georgia were beautiful and well maintained women. Beth looked into her friend's eyes and she felt a connection that surprised her because it made her feel like the happy teenage girl she had been.

Beth was happy now but the happiness then was purer and more open. She suddenly realized that her nasty secret attitude toward Georgia began when Georgia's business succeeded and got worse when Georgia fell in love with the perfect man.

Hank gave Georgia all the freedom she wanted and yet he was there as her biggest fan club when Georgia wanted to try something new.

Married Life

After the usual exchanges and ordering salads with a small glass of white wine, Beth sensed that in spite of all the happiness that Georgia assured her was still part of married life, something was wrong.

So she asked and Georgia looked at her, took a deep breath and said, "How do you feel about sex? I mean, is it important in your life?"

Beth laughed.

What a perfect question to ask. Beth could not stop laughing. She waved a hand at her friend to indicate that she was all right but she could not speak because she was laughing so much.

Then she took a deep breath and put on a serious face, "Why do you ask?"

Georgia was puzzled at Beth's reaction and she had a moment of wondering if Beth was laughing at her. Beth had a hard edge to her sometimes.

Georgia didn't like giving up control in any way, shape or form. Admitting that there might be something wrong in paradise was giving up control.

To tell anyone that there was something missing in her life would give away some of her personal information.

It would give someone an edge over her. But she knew she had to talk about her sexless life to someone and Beth was the logical choice.

The sad fact is that her life was not exactly sexless — it was worse than sexless.

She had tried to email Beth about it more than once but this was not something she wanted to put in writing. That would really make her vulnerable.

"Are you all right?" Beth asked.

Georgia hesitated and then knew that she had to let it spill out. She sometimes sensed that Beth was judgmental about her marriage to Hank and not for the first time, she wondered if Beth were a lesbian.

Georgia wasn't a lesbian but she had a couple of dalliances in the past with women. It was a fantastic release and relief and it was not like cheating on Hank.

The first woman she ended up making love to was some woman she met at a marketing conference. They had started talking during a presentation that was not terribly stimulating and the woman had invited her up to her hotel room for a cocktail.

They laughed and sipped their cocktails and then as the woman was changing into something more comfortable than the power suit she was wearing she asked Georgia to help her with the clasp on the back of her silk top.

It just seemed like the right thing to do to lean forward and kiss her neck once the clasp was undone. When the woman – and Georgia always did this. She always thought of her as "the woman" as if she did not remember her name.

Her name was Kerry Ann.

When Kerry Ann turned, their lips met and Georgia felt her hands skillfully unbutton Georgia's blouse and then release her skirt. Kerry Ann turned around so that her face was at Georgia's waist level and she lowered her head to Georgia's mound.

Her breath was hot through the silk panties and immediately Georgia was damp. Her limbs were light, weightless and it was as if they drifted to the bed.

Georgia didn't remember how they ended up on the bed. She only remembered running her tongue along the smooth lines of Kerry Ann's hipbones and the white smoothness of her rounded buttocks.

The strangeness of burying her face in Kerry Ann's sweetly scented pussy lingered in Georgia's mind long after their passionate evening in bed. For the first time – and the last time – in Georgia's life, she had a spontaneous orgasm.

They were shifting positions and Georgia was thinking how small the bones in Kerry Ann's body felt when they moved their legs so that Georgia's legs were wrapped around one of Kerry Ann's.

A long sleek thigh was pressed against Georgia's clit and it happened. Wave upon wave of hot and cold shudders spread out from her center and the suddenness and completeness took her breath away.

Her heart was racing. The orgasm was like crystal, shimmering and shattering and musical, as it consumed her entire body.

Lost in the sensations, Georgia was no longer aware of what she did and what was done to her. She was lost in a warm ocean of pleasure.

Georgia did not know until that moment that these sensations actually existed. She had been orgasmic, or so she thought, for most of her adult life and she was used to struggling to keep that magic moment held between her thighs for as long as possible.

Every time it flickered intensely but was gone before she was even fully aware that it was there. And that was part of the problem that led her to yield up some of her control to her old buddy Beth.

Sitting across from Beth, Georgia looked at her friend and knew that she had to talk to someone. To Beth. Beth would understand.

"Married life is killing me," Georgia said.

Doing it in the Hallway

They each had a second glass of wine. Beth listened, nodding from time to time. She knew what Georgia meant about the velvet trap of married life.

It was warm and cozy and comfortable but it was so empty and lonely when the evenings came to a close. Hank and Georgia would go to bed and snuggle into their king size bed with the Egyptian cotton sheets and the subdued artwork on the walls.

Hank would reach for her and her nipples would shrivel away from his clumsy touch.

"Tell him," Beth said.

"I can't." Georgia fought back tears. "I don't have the words and even if I did…what would I tell him? Don't do that. Do this?"

She shrugged. "It wouldn't make any difference." She knew it wouldn't. It wasn't just that Hank was boringly awkward in bed, the idea of having sex with him was such a turn off, that Georgia never got wet any more.

Sex hurt. He could rub as much lotion into her vagina as possible, all she felt was messy and uncomfortable. She tried losing herself in thoughts of sex the way she wanted it to be.

"At least it's not hallway sex," Beth said. Georgia looked at her puzzled.

Beth grinned, "You know, where you only see each other in the hallway and say, "fuck you" to each other."

It was a tacky old joke and Georgia was surprised that Beth told it. It was not Beth's sense of humor at all.

"Sorry Georgia," Beth said. "I was just trying to be silly to buy time while I come up with something bright and witty to say."

Beth felt badly for ever having been mean-spirited about Georgia's life. She was smart enough to know that everyone has some burdens to bear. She turned her attention back to what Georgia was telling her and she would see what she could offer in the way of advice.

Georgia was talking about Hank talking. Hank talked. All the time. He explained what he was doing the whole time he was doing it.

She poured out her frustration to Beth. "I am so tired of the painful messy procedure of inserting tab A into slot B."

"I think I'm sexually dead and the worst part is I think about sex all the time. But when I'm in bed, I loathe being touched."

"Have you a thought about having a plain ordinary old affair?" Beth asked.

Georgia looked down at her hands and was quiet for a moment. Then she looked up at Beth and told her about the encounter she had with the woman at the conference.

"Was that when things start to go bad with Hank?" Beth asked.

"No," said Georgia. "Sure, there had been boring moments before that. But it was all right for a while. We were both busy and sex once a week well – it was kind of fun."

Georgia continued, "I thought about it and thought about it. I even wondered if perhaps I would be better off if I had chosen the lesbian lifestyle. But I really couldn't get into that scene."

She knew because she had already tried sex with a woman again, after Kerry Ann. It was satisfying but it was not the explosive and exciting and satisfying experience that she wanted.

The only good thing about it was that it was different from Hank.

She looked away and tried to form the words to explain how she knew that her fantasies and her attraction were definitely heterosexual.

She turned back, "No. I know for a fact that it's really cock that I like."

"How adventuresome is Hank?"

Georgia laughed. "What do you think? Does he sound like Mr. Exciting?"

"Well," Beth grinned, "He doesn't. But he is handsome... and I don't think he was always like this."

Georgia shook her head. "No. He wasn't." She looked at Beth with tears filling her eyes, "I think it's me."

"You?" Beth felt a sense of affection for her old friend. "There is nothing wrong with you – other than the married woman blues."

Then Beth said, "I have an idea. But first, let me tell you about the Curvy Girls."

The Curvy Girls

And she and a couple of her friends had a great solution to their need for top quality sex – on their terms. They had a little club that they called the Curvy Girls.

Curvy girls do it deeper. That's the tagline the Curvy Girls used when they started their club. It was how they billed themselves when they built their first online presence.

The curvy girls' idea solved a problem that every woman has. They could not get enough sex. It started when Amy and Amanda were in graduate school. Beth was already working for a major bank. All three of the women were having a girl gab session one night and realized that they all had the same problem.

They were horny, horny, horny. All they wanted was sex, lots of sex, and good sex. However, they were very very busy and the bar scene just didn't work for any of them.

One of them said, "There's nothing more disgusting than ending up with some guy who's had too much to drink." They agreed that, in spite of what men think, booze does not turn them into handsome, sexy creatures that are capable of imaginative sex.

None of the girls had open schedules and the time to get into all the surrounding crap that goes with the dating and pick up scene.

Beth sometimes remembered that she was the one who came up with the idea but it had become such a casual and yet satisfying idea that she was no longer sure that it was her invention.

She told Georgia about the Curvy Girls in great details.

"We wanted free access to open and unbridled sex when we needed it and had time available."

Beth added, "Some people might say that this is a man's approach to sex – we want what we want when we want it. But the truth is, this is the way all people should think of sex. It's not just for men, you know."

Because Beth was the one with the big modern house and lots of space, the parties were usually held at her place. The other two curvy girls shared an apartment because they were still in graduate school.

That reminded her that she should talk to them about all three of them sharing the house. It only made sense. Beth was rarely home and when she was, it was either a curvy girl party occasion or she was reading in bed.

Neither Amy nor Amanda were home much either because they were just as obsessed with their work as Beth was with hers.

Beth also knew how to play and she played just as hard as she worked. She had plans this weekend to go out to dinner with her friend, Armand.

Organized Fucking

Beth's idea was simple. Georgia and Hank needed to spice up their sex life. They needed to take it beyond the bedroom and Beth didn't mean something as simple as buying a new dildo.

After Beth told Georgia about the curvy girls and how they satisfy their sexual needs by calling on their stable of willing studs for a little impromptu partying, Georgia was dumbfounded.

She was thinking, Beth? Prissy Beth into orgies?

When Beth told her that sometimes all three of them, Amy, Amanda and Beth, got together with three guys or maybe four or five, Georgia just stared at her.

Beth said, "Sometimes we just call one or two of the guys over fun. Basically we're just a gang of good old fuck buddies who like to play."

Georgia got her voice back and interrupted, "well maybe that would satisfy my sexual needs, and trust me right now these are big needs. I spend my whole day thinking about sex and then go home to my hot husband and think maybe tonight's the night."

Georgia felt like she was going to choke. For at least a year, her whole life had been one long series of sexual frustration and orgasms that almost but never quite happened.

Beth said, "You know, we can organize anything you want. Think about it. If you want to come over to one of our parties or if you want to come over as a couple, we could have a good time."

Georgia didn't know how to respond. Beth looked at her friend and said, "You know Georgia, I'm really good at organizing parties. Actually I'm really good at organizing just about anything."

"Plain ordinary old-fashioned wife swapping?" Georgia said. She was imagining telling Hank about this idea. Plain? Old-fashioned.

Beth said, "I'm taking this right out of your hands and I am going to set up something that I don't think will hurt –."

Georgia interrupted, "It couldn't be any worse."

Beth said, "Then it's a deal. Tomorrow night, my place. You and Hank be there at 8 o'clock. I'll have a surprise for you. Both of you."

Once More with Passion

Georgia planned to go along with the idea until their lunch was over and then call it off. But she didn't. Then she planned to call and tell Beth that something came up and they couldn't make it.

She realized that she was just lying to herself. There was no way she was going to miss this get-together.

The hardest part was telling Hank about the party that Beth was organizing. As soon as she mentioned Beth and party in the same sentence, Hank let out a big sigh.

"Oh come on, Georgia, the last thing I want to do on our only free night in town is go spend an evening with Beth."

"I thought you liked Beth," Georgia said.

"I do. I really do like Beth but it's just that I kind of wanted us to do something special. Just you and me." Hank looked at his wife and she saw his expression.

It was a golden opportunity to open the door into that untalked about area. Their personal life. Their marriage. Them. Sex.

"I do love you," Georgia said. And she did. In this moment she knew that they had to do something because Hank was the best man she had ever known.

If she had to choose, she would choose Hank over good sex but she wished she could have both.

"And I really love you," Hank said. Both of them could hear the "but" that hovered at the end of their sentences.

Georgia said it first. "But?" She smiled. She really didn't want to hurt him.

"Yes. But...." Hank made a grimace. Then Georgia realized that she didn't want to be hurt either.

"I think we need to talk," Georgia said. Then she hastily added because she knew what a dreadful phrase that was; it was such a precursor to bad news most of the time, "But it's something good to talk about."

She was nervous.

"I'm listening," Hank said.

Georgia told Hank about the surprise party that Beth was planning – just for them. He stared at her.

"Are you serious?" He said.

"Yes. But only if you are."

"Well, what kind of a party is it going to be?" Hank asked.

"I'm not exactly sure. Sex. I guess."

Hank said, "But you must have some idea."

"All I know is that Beth said to be there at eight. She herself is not going to be involved in the party other than to introduce us to the other guest or guests."

"I don't think I'm going to like this," Hank said.

"Then we don't have to play. We can all sit around and have a civilized glass of wine and brag about our possessions."

"Well I'm not going to go to bed with some other man. I'm not even going to look at another man." Hank sounded indignant but he kept on talking.

"Beth? I always thought she was such a stick in the mud."

Hank pulled Georgia to the bed and began to nibble her neck. She could see his arousal even before he took his clothes off. His cock was rock hard.

He kept on talking anyway. "I love the taste of you," he said. Then he stopped. "Beth? Beth has group sex? Unbelievable."

Then he went back to nibbling Georgia's neck.

Body language, Georgia thought, as she squatted over him and slid down over the full hard length of his cock that was hot and throbbing.

He started talking again, as he always did, describing what was happening.

"I am all the way inside you. I can feel the heat of you and your wetness running down over my balls…."

Georgia bounced up and down on his hard cock feeling it stretch her insides she leaned forward stretching her legs out behind her and pressing her breasts against his chest.

If she rocked herself up and down in this position, her clit rubbed against his pubic bone bringing her to an orgasm that was stronger than usual.

Hank thrust against her and then when he felt her orgasm begin to diminish he put his hands on her hips and used his powerful arms to lift her back into the position where she was sitting on top of his cock.

He held her hips immobile as he thrusted himself up and into her over and over until he sprayed her with his full load.

Georgia was pleased and she drifted into a well-fucked sleep. She thought that perhaps they didn't need to go to Beth's. Then as she finally drifted into sleep, she was thinking that if just the thought of going to Beth brought this reaction from Hank then what would the real thing do.

Getting Down and Dirty

Less than twenty-four hours later Georgia knew what the real thing did. It opened a door into a world she never knew existed.

It began as a typical party. Beth introduced Georgia and Hank to her friend Amy and guy named William. Amy was the exact opposite in appearance to Beth and Georgia.

Her coloring was darker, she was shorter and she was more round, completely curvaceous. Hank could see her full breasts and he felt nervous and excited.

He didn't know what was about to happen but he had a pretty good idea that before long he would have those round firm globes under his hands and in his mouth.

Georgia was almost quivering with anticipation but she had no idea where to start, or even what to say. Did they go into a bedroom and if so did they all go into the same bedroom or did they pair off.

If they paired off, did they pair off as the couples they were and then separate? Did Amy expect to have sex with Georgia?

Shortly after she made the introductions, Beth said, "Amy knows where everything is. Enjoy yourselves. I'm going out for the evening."

Beth knew that a fifth wheel would not add anything to the party and besides she had her own private fun scheduled at her part-time boyfriend's place. She was right in the mood to paddle Armand's bum.

Beth had a special relationship that involved a special kind of attention which she liked to administer to him. Her special fuck buddy, Armand, was not really a fuck buddy.

Armand liked to be spanked. He liked a good hard spanking, preferably with a leather belt. He was not interested in anything other than being spanked and he could achieve orgasm only this way. Beth enjoyed spanking him.

It was a great way to take the edge off her when she was feeling tense. Armand was also a lot of fun for her to spend time with because they had the same taste in music and plays.

Beth said her goodbyes and made Georgia promise to call her in the morning. Amy became a gracious hostess instantly and said, "I understand you are new at this."

She was speaking to both Georgia and Hank.

Georgia said, "Yes."

Amy explained, "There are no set rules except that we all must have fun. No one has to do anything they don't want to do or feel uncomfortable doing."

She said, "We should pick a safe word and the second something is making you uncomfortable, you just holler out that word and we'll stop."

Hank suggested, "Cucumber."

The word was too long, Georgia said.

"Then we'll say cuke," Hank suggested.

"No," William said, "that sounds too much like cock."

They finally settled on carrot as the safe word.

Amy then said, "I think the first thing to do is for us to get comfy."

She reached over and picked up a brightly colored large cotton wrap from the end table. She handed it to Georgia. Georgia shook it open. It was a very pretty wrap that was about five feet square.

As Georgia looked at it, Amy picked up a bright blue wrap and shook it open. Amy then began to shed her clothes. She stacked her folded clothes neatly on the chair where Beth had been sitting.

She had full round buttocks and extremely large breasts with nipples that were deep red and hard. Her bush was trimmed and shaped like a heart.

Amy pulled the blue wrap around her body and tied it in a knot between her breasts. William meanwhile was draping his clothes over the back of the chair where Beth sat.

He was shorter than Hank with very broad shoulders and finely sculpted biceps and thigh muscles. His penis was thick, almost as big around as a soda can and it was standing at full mast.

Hank stood up and took off his shirt. Then he pulled off his socks and dropped his trousers. Georgia looked at his body and realized that he was in fine shape.

His cock was not as thick as Williams but it was longer by almost an inch.

Amy came toward Georgia and began to help her undress. William was behind her nibbling on the back of her neck and cupping her breasts in his large hands.

She could feel his cock pressing against the small of her back.

Georgia was aware of Amy pulling Hank towards them so that he was standing almost between Amy and Georgia.

Maybe she was clutching for some touchstone, some link to the familiar but Georgia began to wonder if Hank would start describing the action.

It would not be possible. There was so much action that all seemed to take place at once. Suddenly they were in a huddle of naked flesh against naked flesh, hands everywhere.

Georgia could feel two cocks against her and she put her hands on Amy's firm young breasts and felt William's smooth muscles.

There were fingers in her vagina and lips on her nipples and a hand stroking her ass. Lips on her lips, lips on her neck, lips on her labia.

Then she was lifted and carried to the sofa where she was enveloped in flesh.

She floated and felt full and complete. There was no beginning and no end to the bodies that were touching. They moved into the bedroom.

Georgia's feet did not touch the ground. The men carried her into the bedroom and laid her on the bed, with Hank spreading one leg, pulling it toward him, kissing her inner thigh.

Amy pulled her other leg toward her and William was between her legs, his thick hard penis pressing into her wet and willing cunt.

He slid it into her, smoothly and easily and swiftly. Hank's mouth was on her breast, his teeth nipping at her turgid pointed nipple.

Georgia could see the look of love on Hank's face as he watched her face contort in ecstasy.

"Suck me, please," Hank said as he moved to bring his cock, already beaded with pre-cum to her mouth. Georgia held his balls in her hand and took the head of his cock into her mouth while waves of pleasure wafted over her and through her.

Let's Do it like We Used To

Hank watch his wife wrap her legs around William and watch William's muscular ass bunch and relax over and over as he plunged into Georgia and then pulled out and plunged into her again.

He had watched his share of porn over the years but it was never as good as this.

His first thought was that he would die of jealousy if he saw some other man fuck his wife but he didn't feel jealousy at all. He felt like he was part of this whole game and he loved it.

He felt closer to Georgia than he had ever felt and he was watching a complete stranger with a huge cock fuck her until she moaned in ecstasy.

Married sex had become routine and matter of fact and while it was an act of love, it was not as exciting as it could be. Sometimes it even felt like a duty.

He looked at Amy and realized that he had not actually touched her magnificent globes. He had looked at them when she was undressing but since then, it had been a series of body parts and touching and nibbling but in all of that, he had not touched Amy's tits, not deliberately.

Georgia was sucking his cock. Hank leaned over and took one of Amy's ample nipples in his mouth and sucked catching the nipple between his tongue and the roof of his mouth.

Then he took her entire breast in both his hands and kneaded and squeezed. The sensation was exquisite. Amy guided him to her side of the bed. They were each on one side of William and Georgia who were entwined in a routine rutting rhythm.

Amy brought Hank around and used her hips to nudge him on to his back. She leaned over him, her body poised above his cock, her huge tits tickling his chest and then she slid the length of her warm wet pussy over his throbbing cock.

He turned his head to his left saw Georgia's face just inches away from him. He kissed his wife who was being jounced with the rapid thrusts of William who was clearly about to shoot his load.

William suddenly moved up and over Georgia and sprayed his white jism all over her belly and breasts, his glistening cock, shooting jet after jet of his juices.

Hank felt his own load about to let go and he clutched Amy's round ass in his hands as she rode him into oblivion.

The Family That Plays Together

Hours later, completely drained, Hank and Georgia returned to their hotel room. They took a shower together, gently washing each other's backs and other body parts.

They were both unusually silent but the dynamic tension between them spoke volumes. Each of them knew that something wonderful had happened this evening.

Georgia, whose consulting business relied on her articulate way with words, was surprised at the realization that body language was so powerful. She was grateful because she could not think of anything to say.

Somehow thinking about their evening in terms of body language made her giggle like a schoolgirl. She was stretched out naked on the bed, her hair still damp from the shower when she started to giggle.

She didn't care that her hair would be completely messed up and tousled and unruly because she didn't blow it dry before getting into bed.

Hank got into bed beside her and stretched out on his back. They lay side-by-side holding hands and gazing at the ceiling.

Hank was prone to over talking about everything, at least that's how Georgia thought of his analytical approach to life – over talking. Tonight he hardly spoke.

Hank was lost for words. It was as simple as that. Georgia was surprised to realize that she missed his talking. It was part of the way they were.

Georgia was at first one to break the silence and all she could think to say was, "wow."

Hank said, "I never would have imagined that we would do such a thing."

"Me either." She had not achieved the same kind of orgasm that she had with Kerry Ann but she had achieved several other types of orgasms. Most of them better than the one with Kerry Ann.

Georgia was about to ask if he regretted having done it but realized that was not the kind of question that would be right to ask at this moment.

There was nothing to regret and she didn't want to plant the idea in his head that maybe she regretted it. Because she sure didn't.

"I thought it would be different," Georgia said. "I never thought I would get turned on watching you screw somebody else."

Hank rolled over to the side and laid a hand on her belly. "I felt the same way. But it was the weirdest thing, the way I felt, when I saw that guy with that incredible Dick of his, stick it into you."

"I got to see all of it, the way your pussy lips opened and the look of a cock disappearing into you, and his balls slapping against your ass hole."

Hank continued, "I see all of you, every square inch of your body. And I feel the heat of you when I enter you. But it was like fucking you myself to see him fuck you."

Georgia said, "I think maybe the whole thing about being jealous is if you were fucking somebody and I wasn't there, I'd be excluded. I'd be left out. But I was part of it – watching you give and get pleasure while I was giving and getting too."

She was trying to find the words to explain how sharing this experience with him, even though there were other people in the room and in the bed, made her feel closer to him.

"This is something we're going to have to do again," Hank said.

Georgia smiled as she drifted into sleep. She had been thinking the exact same thing.

Curvy Girls Do It On Vacation
Vacation!!

Amanda was done.

Done.

The last report was handed in. The last class over.

She was going on vacation. Yay. She was going to go someplace quiet and peaceful. Right now she had enough of people to do her a lifetime. Well, for at least a month.

She'd had one last party with Beth and Amy the night before and that sex would have to do her for the duration of her stay in the deep woods in Maine.

The guy she hooked up with was great. The usual Curvy Girls' party had great looking guys but the last night party was special.

The Curvy Girls were the nickname that she and Amy and Beth applied to themselves. Three slightly bent women with high sex drives and not enough time to deal with all the social niceties such as dating and social events. They stripped down their needs to the basics.

Good sex with fun-loving, well-endowed men who were available to party in the odd hours of life. Like ten o'clock at night. "Come on over for some fun," they would text the guys and they would meet at Beth's and fuck for a couple of hours.

No emotional ties or games. Just good sex.

Best of all, whatever a girl wanted, she could get. Amanda loved being on top and she loved having her pussy licked. She was not a big fan of doggie style fucking but Amy was.

If the guy wanted to pound his cock in from behind, she would suggest a swap with Amy. Amy loved it rough from behind and if the guy took extra long strokes and his cock happened to pull out of Amy's juicy pussy and make a slight adjustment and end up poking into her nether regions, that was fine with Amy.

She loved taking it up the ass. But for some reason it was even better for her if the ass fucking was sudden and unplanned. There were a couple of their regular fuck buddies who knew this about Amy and made a point of surprising her this way.

Amanda was surprised at how much she learned about her own likes and dislikes in the Curvy Girls' parties.

She had never known the freedom of asking for and getting exactly what she wanted in bed until she started playing this game with her friends. It extended into her personal life as well.

Not that sex was not her personal life but she meant her life with her professors and her colleagues. It was so much more efficient to say what was on her mind. It saved on misunderstandings and it saved her from a lot of wasted time doing crap she didn't want to do.

Last night she was in a mood to be licked for hours. The guy who was her primary partner for the evening was a guy named Greg. He started by kissing her ankles and worked up one leg and inner thigh and then turned his attention to the other leg and inner thigh, each time approaching her open cunt with the promise of sucking her clitoris as if it were a tiny lollipop.

She was squirming with anticipation by the time he buried his face in her damp pussy. He took her round ass in his hands and clutched her cheeks firmly pulling her center closer to his face.

While Greg sucked and nibbled her tender parts, the other two men at the party came into the bedroom and kneeled one on each side of her and simultaneously took a breast and began to suckle.

It was heaven. This was what she wanted more than anything. This complete attention to the points of the magic triangle of her sexuality. Penetration was all right and it felt good but having a man at each breast and another licking her labia and sucking her clit was so much more comprehensive and encompassing. Sex was never like this before.

She didn't have to struggle to reach a climax. She could let it just happen and it was so much better when it built up slowly and steadily, in a series of wave like lappings until it reached a crescendo of pleasure that was so intense it almost made her faint.

Now it was morning and she was already in her rented car rolling down the highway. It was a long drive but the drive was part of the relaxation. She had her music playing and in the car she could drive along singing at the top of her lungs.

In the Woods

It was late afternoon when she arrived in the small town that was really nothing more than a wide spot in the road. There was a restaurant that was also a gas station and a convenience store.

Amanda parked her car and went into the restaurant. She decided to have a decent snack of comfort food. Whatever the special was, she would have that for her dinner. Then she would pick up some supplies and follow the instruction to get to the cabin that one of her professors had managed to get for her for the month.

Once she got to check out the place, she would decide what she really needed and find her way to Bangor for some serious grocery shopping.

Or maybe there was a small town – a real town – somewhere nearer than Bangor which had to be at least an hour away.

She would need fruit and veggies and yogurt. All the necessities of life. She stopped her thoughts for a moment. No – she had to be accurate.

Food and water and sex were the necessities of life for her and the sexual escapade at Beth's house last night would have to satisfy her for a month. It was nothing new for her to go a month without sex.

But she was on vacation. She was resting up after the long hard work in graduate school. Her thought had been to unwind in the relaxing Maine woods, dreaming of her future, finding the strengths she had and getting rid of the weaknesses.

It was supposed to be a cerebral time.

But now that she was almost at the cabin, she began to wonder if perhaps she really needed that much tranquility in her life.

She went into the restaurant part of the business and ordered a coffee and a cinnamon roll. What decadence. A huge sugary cinnamon roll for dinner.

It was good and tasty and Amanda had two more cups of coffee. The waitress was about Amanda's age – mid-twenties. She was big-bosomed and wore a very snug uniform, the type that Amanda had never seen in real life. It was the type that she might have seen in a movie set in the 1950s.

The uniform was pale blue and of some sort of synthetic fabric that would repel water and just about anything else. The waitress had her hair piled up on top of her head in an elaborate bun.

She looked like she was from central casting. Her name was embroidered on the breast of her uniform in curly letters. Madge.

"Thank you Madge," Amanda said.

The waitress laughed. "I'm not really Madge."

"Oh," Amanda said. She looked at the name on the uniform.

"Doncha love it?" The waitress said. "I got this at a yard sale. It fit me pretty good and it's so easy to wash. Just one of those old wash and wear jobbies. And it get me great tips from the old guys."

"It's a classic." Amanda said.

"Thank you," said the waitress. "My real name's Kim."

"Nice name," Amanda said.

"You just passing through?" Kim asked.

Amanda was about to say yes, she was but she knew that chances were good that she would see Kim again and it was not a great idea to start out with a lie that would so easily be discovered.

Besides, so what if some people knew she was staying here for a few weeks. Tourism was a major source of industry for the rural area. Maine was beautiful in a rugged sort of way and the reason cabins like the one she would be staying at existed.

"I'm staying at the MacLure cabin."

Kim raised her eyebrows and made a small pursed look with her lips. "Verrrryyyy nice."

"I haven't seen it yet," Amanda said.

"Oh wow. You will love it." Kim said with a big smile. Then she added, "Do you know how to get to it?"

"I have a map and a GPS."

"Then you should have no problem. But if you do, just call me." Kim wrote her phone number on her order pad and passed it to Amanda.

"Mom might answer but I'll tell her about you." Then Kim laughed, "I guess I should get your name."

As it turned out, Amanda had no trouble finding the place. The only thing that surprised her was that it was not a cabin but a huge log mansion. It sprawled over the property which was surrounded by tall trees.

It was off a road that was off a road that was off the main road. Not a complicated path but someone would have to really go out of their way to get to it.

Amanda thought it would be a great place to hide if she actually wanted to get away from society and become a hermit.

As it was, it was luxurious without any of the annoying tourist things that Amanda disliked. Things such as noisy people in the lobby. Things like people playing music that was distracting.

There was a den with a wide selection of music and a whole wall of bookshelves. Some of the books were popular fiction novels, not Amanda's first choice in reading but it would be fun to explore some of them.

The house seemed to have endless rooms but that was part of the design where rooms led into other rooms. And before long, Amanda was thinking about the parties they could have in this cabin in the woods.

Day One

The first day began as heavenly as Amanda could imagine. She woke up with the first momentary feeling of panic, like she had forgotten to do something really important. Then it passed.

She had no deadlines, no meetings, no classes, no seminars. She didn't even have to have lunch with anyone. She could stay in her pajamas all day long if she liked.

It was marvelous. She loved it. She nibbled on cheese and grapes that she had packed for the trip and listened to the birds in the trees.

She napped several times. She did nothing all day long except remind herself that she was a free being and no thought was needed.

Day Two

Day two was the same and she loved it. In the afternoon, it happened. She stretched out naked on the deck. It was early summer and the day was warm, even for Maine.

She was on the exercise mat which was not as comfortable as the lounge chair. Her plan was to try to meditate and she did not want to be so comfortable that she would fall asleep.

But she did.

It was a sudden deep sleep and she was in an embrace that did not make any sense. She could smell his scent which was like pine and like sweet sweat and like cinnamon. And she felt his fingers on her pussy.

She did not see his face and her attention was on his fingers which were playing with her nub and her pussy lips and it was like he had her entire sensual pleasure captured in his fingertips.

Her skin tingled. Waves of pleasure rippled from her navel to her knees and she felt her breasts expand to press against the chest of her unseen dream lover.

Her orgasm started slowly and it spread like hot blood through her body, slowly and then quickly with the intensity growing and growing at her core.

The feeling did not rise to a crescendo and then dissipate. It rose to a crescendo but it kept rising until her nerves were on fire and the pleasure was close to pain.

The fingers never left her center and she never saw his face but she did not even notice that no penis touched her or penetrated her.

She was all sexual intensity, her breasts as sensitive as her clit, her nipples, her thighs, her arms – all of her on fire.

She was breathless and wondering if she could take any more pleasure before it turned to pain.

Then she woke. The waves of her immense orgasm were still simmering in her body when she woke, the bright sun shining down on her face, her body.

She had tears in her eyes, she could feel the wetness on her cheeks and running down into her hair. She struggled to sit up and bring her mind back to the reality that surrounded her.

She was confused. She was not sure where she was and where her lover went and then she understood that it was a dream.

The dream left her completely drained but in a good way. She tried to recall the dream but as the day went on the dream faded and all she could remember was the sensation of her climax that was broader and deeper than possible in real life.

Except that it had happened in real life. The sensations might have been started by the dream lover who was not real and who did not exist but the results were very real.

Enough is Never Enough

The first week of the vacation was everything that Amanda imagined. She loved the pure air and the Jacuzzi and the shade of the trees and the freedom to lounge around the back deck without a stitch of clothes on.

The dream orgasm was intense enough to drain Amanda of any sexual needs. She had wondered how it would feel when she knew that there would be no sex in her life for the month she was away.

It was one thing to forgo sex when she was too busy to think about it but here in her hideaway cabin, she had nothing to distract her.

She found a book that fascinated her and she read it entirely from cover to cover in two days even though it was a very thick book.

After she finished the book, she realized that there was no food in the house. She had eaten the snacks she brought with her and the food that she had picked up at the convenience store.

It was after ten in the evening and she looked at the listings in the phone book but there was no way to tell much about the offerings. The addresses meant nothing to her and none of them offered delivery.

She didn't see any taxi listings in the area so she couldn't call a cab to deliver a pizza for her. The small map she had of the area showed that the roads were easy to navigate.

Amanda went out for a drive. The night was dark and there were few lights on in the houses she saw along the way. When she got to the main road, she saw that nothing was open. Not even the convenience store attached to the restaurant.

There was no place to find a midnight snack. Or even a ten p.m. snack.

Amanda drove back to the cabin, feeling just a little bit frustrated and more than a little bit frisky. There was something about the country air and the knowledge that all around her there were people living their lives but she was alone in the world.

She wondered if a time would come when she would have enough of this peace and quiet and the entire freedom from pressure.

She had also wondered the same thing about the dream sex – would it ever be possible to have enough sex to last forever or at least for a very long time.

At this moment, she realized that enough was never enough. It could be enough for the moment but soon memory would start to fragment and the feelings would have to be reactivated.

The only way to reactivate the feeling was by reliving the moment or some variation of the moment.

Bacon and Eggs

Amanda was planning to sleep in even though she had gone to bed shortly after her drive. Part of her was hoping that the sleep would bring back another of her fabulous erotic dreams.

She was awakened at eight by the sound of a vehicle pulling into the yard. She peeked out the bedroom window and saw a big red pickup truck park.

A broad-shouldered man with a blue plaid shirt tucked into his straight-legged jeans got out of the truck. Amanda watched him reach back in and take out a brown paper bag.

He carried it to the front door. She waited to hear the doorbell ring. Then she realized that she didn't know if there was a doorbell.

No one but her was there so there had never been an occasion for the doorbell to be needed. She listened for the sound of a knock.

No sound.

Then she saw the man go back to the truck, empty-handed, and get into the cab. The truck door shut and the big vehicle drove away.

Amanda pulled on her housecoat and went downstairs to see what he had done with the bag. From the angle of her bedroom window, she could only see part of the front deck.

She opened the front door. The bag was sitting on the deck beside of the door. There was a note sticking out of it.

"Hi Amanda,

I saw you drove by the restaurant last night after we closed. I figured you might be hungry so here are some things you might like.

If you like bacon and eggs, we do breakfast until 11 a.m.

Kim"

Bacon and eggs?

Amanda picked up the bag and brought it into the house. Yogurt, oranges, a loaf of homemade bread and a bottle of jam.

She ate an orange and was looking for a knife to slice the bread.

Bacon and eggs sounded really good.

Amanda drove into the restaurant. Kim came over to the table to take her order and Amanda thanked her for the groceries and offered to reimburse her for them.

Kim waved her away. "It was just the neighborly thing to do," she said.

Amanda ordered a classic breakfast, which is how it was described on the menu. It was a huge breakfast. She ate slowly and enjoyed every bite.

Once she finished her breakfast and tipped Kim well, Amanda went to the grocery store which was not very large but which did carry a good wide variety of goods. She stocked up.

After a pleasant tour of the area, Amanda went back to the cabin.

When she had packed away the groceries, she realized that she was just a little bit lonely. It was the curse of being human, she thought.

Too many people all the time got on her nerves, especially when she was trying to work. But she wasn't trying to work. This was unusual for her, not to have a pile of work to do.

But too few people also got on her nerves, she realized. And this was a dilemma for her. She didn't want to have someone come and visit her even for a couple of days. She knew that once someone was there and they had talked for a couple of hours, she would regret having them there.

So calling Amy and suggesting she come for the weekend would not be a good idea. In any case, Amy was up to her ears in the final work on her thesis and would be too busy to come.

Beth would be just as busy with work.

Amanda went through the list of the other people she knew. She realized that part of the problem was not just loneliness – she was horny.

She had tried to recreate the dream a couple of times, stretching out nude on the deck but it had not been as warm as it had been that first time she did her nude deck dreaming.

Masturbation was always a great solution and before the Curvy Girls had invented themselves she had indulged in self-pleasure quite a bit.

She pinched her nipples with the fingers of one hand while she tried to recreate the way that the dream man had grasped her tender pussy flesh, squeezing her clit and cunt lips with the thumb and first three fingers of the other hand.

It was pleasurable. She had a gentle and almost satisfying come.

Later she tried another session with herself, this time with a cucumber. It was a long skinny English cucumber with a slight curve. She propped herself up on a couple of pillows and slid the green vegetable into herself, letting it graze her passion bud as she thrust her hips up to meet the cuke.

The second orgasm was deeper and more satisfying and she dozed after.

One of Amanda's fantasies was having sex with a big man – a tall man – who would be able to manhandle her into a lot of unusually positions and who she would be able to climb aboard and ride without worrying about whether she was putting too much weight on his stomach or smothering with her tits.

She also suspected that a really big man would have really big equipment. The skinny cucumber was a mistake, she thought. She wanted something thick shoved inside her.

Something wide and stiff that would spread her cunthole wide open and give her that intense sensation that she was about to be split in two.

She thought about going back to the grocery store to get just such a cucumber. Or maybe a small zucchini.

She would put that on her list for tomorrow. Her solution to her loneliness was to get out every day and do sometime – even if it was nothing more than a trip to the vegetable aisle in the grocery store.

She found another book and read it until she fell asleep. When she woke, she knew she had had a dream about sex because she recognized the aftermath of an erotic dream.

But she could not remember what it was about. All she remembered was that she woke in the final throes of a small climax.

Ah Memories

Something that Amanda had wondered before was about the parties at Beth's and how they would affect her in the long run.

How would she be if she were living with a man or married? As it was, when they had several guys over, they shared. They all knew what each other liked best and if they had a guy who was particularly fond of one of their favorites, they swapped.

Amanda loved being completely consumed by sex. Two men were one of the more pleasurable events that took place at Beth's and it was a bit of a routine pleasure for Amanda when there was that switchover where the man who was fucking her gave way to the new player.

For a few minutes or sometimes longer, she had one man in her and one man giving her tits the rough treatment she liked. Or a cock in her pussy and one in her mouth.

She thought that a very large man might be able to give her the same sensation as two men because he would completely envelope her in his body.

He would be big enough to fuck her and take her breasts, one in each huge hand and rock her to the sensations she craved.

She knew that it was always possible to find the kind of person who could give the pleasure that each woman wanted in her own particular way.

She thought about Beth and Armand. Armand had joined the party one evening and ended up showing Beth how she like to spank him.

He loved having his ass paddled until it was a deep pink. Over the months, an affection developed between Beth and Armand and while he never came to the parties anymore, he did spend a lot of time alone with Beth.

Amanda could tell that the Curvy Girls would soon disband or maybe just morph into something else. Other members would start to come to the parties.

Right now, it was just the three of them who attended the gatherings. Her and Beth and Amy.

Although the male players changed all the time, many of them were regulars.

Until they found a partner and wanted more than just wild unfettered sex and they drifted away to live a different lifestyle.

Amanda supposed that if she found a job that took her to another city, someone else would become the third Curvy Girl. Maybe Beth and Amy would continue on, just the two of them. That could be fun too.

About a quarter of the time, only two of them partied. Sometimes they partied at the apartment that Amanda and Amy shared.

It was just more fun when it was the three of them. And it was more fun at Beth's simply because she had bigger beds and more space.

Five men were the best number but that didn't happen often. Four men was also a good number.

Amanda had speculated about starting up a new gang of horny girls if she moved. There were always horny ladies around who needed the time and space to explore their sexuality to the fullest.

Each of them – Beth, Amy and herself – had introduced friends of theirs to the parties and arranged for some spectacular one on one sessions.

People read about sex and tried to find the ultimate sexual experience and they watched movies and they hoped that someone else would find the key to unlock their true passion pit that lurked inside them.

But the only real way to get to the essence of what turned you on, Amanda was convinced, was to let yourself go in the pure pleasures of your own body and the bodies of other willing and playful partners.

She had boyfriends over the years and the first moments of passion were exciting but it seemed to be a habit that they all had – once they had sex two or three times, they settled into a pattern.

It was as if the strokes they took the first time they brought Amanda to orgasm were their tried and true methods of inflicting pleasure.

Some of them never tried anything beyond their first moves and licks and strokes. These were either the ones that they liked best or the ones that they thought Amanda liked best and those were the ones they stayed with.

Until only the emotions they felt for each other continued and the passion faded. Sex became perfunctory.

And how awful was that?

At the parties, the men all tried to be on their best and more creative behavior. After all, there were other people around and no man wanted to climb on one of the women and spend the whole encounter with the simple old thrust and stroke.

They had to use their best moves, their best arrangement of ankles around their necks, their best roll from being on top to being under the woman.

Amanda loved it when they demonstrated their artistry with their tongues. Some flicked. Some sucked. Some licked. Some had a combination of tongue moves that took in everything between her legs.

Some men loved to play with asses. Amanda was surprised at the nerve endings in her ass cheeks. One of her favorite recent experiences involved her sitting on one guy's thick cock, slowing sliding up and down while another guy massaged her ass with his big hands.

He moved slowly and used his fingers to administer small pinches that were not tight pinches but gentle tiny squeezes followed by a smooth finger massage.

He had a hand working on each cheek, bringing out sensations that were astounding in their intensity. He handled her buttocks when she bounced ferociously on the penis and she was lost in the shivers and waves that ran up and down her spine.

Nature Girl

Amanda's wave of loneliness passed and she began to go for long walks along the pathways through the wooded area around her.

There were other cottages in the area but they were just as big as the one where Amanda was staying. Each one was on acres of land and there were long walks between them. They were not connected by actual paths although there were paths.

These paths led to the river or to open areas. However, the trees had open areas that allowed Amanda to wander among them, watching squirrels jump from tree to tree.

She didn't go near the other cottages and she set the location of her own cabin on her phone's GPS so that she could always find her way back to her place.

It would be easy to get lost in these woods. It was not like getting lost in a gigantic wooded area, she thought, because there were other places in almost all directions but it could be uncomfortable if she wandered too far off and started walking in circles.

Let's face it, she said to herself. She was a city girl. What if she saw a moose? Or a bear? She didn't want to get too far from home base.

The walks were energizing and relaxing and Amanda loved the rhythms of her days.

It was a Saturday when she was out for a walk along a path that was by now familiar to her. It led to the river. Amanda loved the sound of the water rolling over the rocks and she planned to sit and read for a while.

She was barely settled in with her bottle of water and a good book that she was nearly finished reading when she heard something.

It was not the usual woodland sounds she had become familiar with. She hoped it was not a bear. Whatever it was, it was bigger than a squirrel.

She kept on reading. Or pretending to read. If she ignored it, maybe it would ignore her. But her heart was pounding. She knew that any animal could smell the fear on her and in her.

What was she thinking? Wandering in the woods like this. Then she had a worse thought. She had seen too many slasher movies in her day and thought, what if this was some sort of madman?

The noise suddenly stopped and Amanda was about to stand up and turn around, frantically wondering if she should move at all. Maybe she should just fall over and play dead.

Then she heard a voice.

"Hello."

A man's voice.

"Hello," she said. Then she slowly stood up and turned around.

"I'm sorry I disturbed you," the man said.

"It's a big woods," she said. "I think we can share it."

He smiled at her and Amanda was rooted to the ground where she stood. He was the biggest man she had ever seen. He had to be at least six and a half feet tall and proportionately built.

He stepped closer to her and held out a hand, "Derek."

She took his hand, "Amanda."

Derek was staying at one of the cottages, he explained and was out for a nature walk. He had come to the cottage for a week's vacation.

He needed to get away from the city from time to time and this was his retreat.

He always came up for a week before they started coming for the summer, bringing their children who were all out of school by then.

"You don't bring your children here." Amanda said and then realized how trite that was, as if she was the typical single woman checking out the availability of the handsome man with the remarkable blue eyes.

He grinned. "No kids." He caught her eyes and they locked, looking deep into each other. Then he added, "I'm single."

Oh the mating rituals of the human being, Amanda thought. She hated man-woman games. What was she supposed to say now? "So am I?

How about "So am I, let's get it on?"

She ended up saying, "Isn't this a gorgeous place?"

They talked about the river and the trees and the vegetation and then he suggested that perhaps she would like to come back to his place for a glass of wine.

She said she would like that.

He suggested that she stay for a barbecue.

"I'd take you out for dinner," he said, "but there aren't too many places around."

"I noticed," she said.

"The restaurant is pretty good," he said. "If you like good old down home cooking."

"Which I do," he added. "But I don't like to drink and drive and I'd like to finish this bottle with you." He poured their third glass of wine.

"I hope I can drink and walk," she said.

"Where are you staying?" he asked.

She told him.

"Ah, I know the way," he said. "I can walk you home safely after dinner."

It was nearly midnight when that happened. Dinner was excellent and the easy conversation was even better. Derek was smart and funny.

When he got her to her cabin, he looked down at her and smiled. "Here you are, safe and sound."

Amanda knew that the goodnight kiss was coming and she was relaxed and ready. The walk home had been completely dark. It was a moonless night and she knew that she never would have been able to walk through the woods in that kind of dark.

Even with the flashlight that Derek carried, she would have been scared. It was so dark she could barely see the trees. As it was she could barely see him. She had not left on any lights because it was no where near dark when she went for her walk.

She opened the door behind her and reached in for the light switch and suddenly they were bathed in light.

The light also broke the spell.

"You didn't lock the door?" he asked.

"I just went for a walk," she said. "I don't bother to lock it for a little walk like that. But I do lock it at night."

"It is pretty safe here," he said.

Saying good night was harder than they realized but eventually they did. He did kiss her good night, holding her in his arms and letting the kiss linger.

"Wow," she whispered. The word escaping her lips.

It was three days and two more barbecues before she said another "wow." She had thought it several times. Once when they went for a drive in the country and he showed her some sights she had only seen in photos before.

Another time when he kissed her good night again the second night they spent talking.

Now she was saying "Wow" because they were in her bedroom and he was taking off his clothes. Her question was answered. This big man was built proportionately.

His cock was a good ten inches long and thick.

He walked toward her, where she was sitting on the side of the bed, his apparatus bobbing slightly with each step.

She spread her legs so that as he reached the high bed, he could walk between her legs. She felt his cock against her moist opening and then he reached around and took her ass in his big hands and lifted her toward him, shoving himself deep inside her.

Amanda wrapped her legs around him and another question was answered. For Amanda, this one man gave her the pleasure of two, as he enveloped her in a world of passion that was as good as sex with two men. Or maybe three.

Curvy Girls Do It Harder with Rock Stars

Good Old Days

Amanda was back from vacation and she still had a lot of free time on her hands. However, the good news was that on vacation she learned how to deal with free time. It was there to be enjoyed.

She was reading more and enjoying it more and spending time with people that she hadn't talked to in years. Not a lot of time, but more time than she had since she started graduate school.

When Amanda was in high school, one of the friends she hung around with was a geeky guy named Kenny. She and Kenny had been in grade school together and he was a bit of a loner.

Just like she was. All Kenny knew about was music. All Amanda cared about was reading. Somewhere along the line, Amanda couldn't really remember exactly when, but they started hanging out together.

A lot of their hanging out together was a form of self-defense. One geek could easily become a victim of bullying. Two geeks form a network and somehow Kenny and Amanda escaped the usual hell of high school.

Once Amanda got lost in college and then her research and graduate school she kept in touch with Kenny usually by email. She didn't exactly live under a rock so she was aware that Kenny had done well for himself in the music world.

It just wasn't her kind of music. Kenny was her kind of people but he was into hard rock and she was more of a Beethoven person.

It was a funny kind of situation, being in touch with Kenny. She literally had not laid eyes on him since they graduated from high school. But when he called her they would pick up the conversation right where they left off.

For Amanda, Kenny would always be that skinny little redhead in grade one. Even in high school he was still a skinny little redhead. He was lean and lanky and hadn't yet grown into his hands and nose. While she was on vacation she got an email from Kenny who said he would be in town and want to know if they could get together for a drink. She emailed him back and said sure.

"All you have to do is name the place," she said. He said he would prefer if she named the place so here she was in their friendly neighborhood bar, waiting for Kenny.

He showed up, the same old Kenny. Taller and if possible, skinnier. He was wearing extremely tight pants in a bold black and white vertical stripe. The pants were topped by a skinny, sleeveless black tank top.

His hair was as red as ever and spiked. He was in his KY Jam get up.

KY Jam

The waitress came to the table to take the order. Amanda knew the waitress fairly well because this was about the only place she had ever come for a drink and she'd been doing that for nearly five years.

The waitress whose name was Sherry smiled at Amanda and then turned to look at Kenny. She opened her mouth and closed it again and then opened it and stood there, slack-jawed, looking at Kenny.

"Oh my God. Oh my God."

Amanda said to Kenny, "Do you want to stay here?"

Kenny looked directly back at the waitress and said, "If I can get a beer."

The waitress nodded but she didn't move.

Amanda said to the waitress, "I'd like a beer too. Bring us whatever's on draft."

The waitress could barely break away long enough to get the beer and when she came back it was clear that she had spread the word. The place was filling up and the noise was increasing.

Amanda laughed, "Kenny, Kenny, Kenny. We might as well go back to my place. It is impossible to get any peace and quiet here."

When Amanda went off to college, Kenny and his best musical friend Greg decided to bypass the academic world and go directly for their dream.

They were going to be rock stars.

There were thousands, maybe millions, of people with the same dream. They would take their talents to the public. Some of them ended up playing in nightclubs in their area of the world.

A few, like Kenny and Greg, find the secret to success. They hooked up with Zeke and Jimbo and managed to be in the right place at the right time.

Within two years, KY Jam was on the cover of *Rolling Stone*. Everywhere they went, crowds of screaming girls appeared.

When they were back in the apartment, Amanda continued to tease Kenny about his popularity with the girls. In high school it was the main topic of Kenny's conversation. Girls hated him. He loved girls.

Kenny was one person. KY Jam was another and Kenny had explained before to Amanda that while KY Jam got all the attention, Kenny was still awkward with girls.

"Oh come on Kenny. Don't try to tell that you're not surrounded by groupies."

"It didn't say I didn't get sex. It's just so boring. It's not like a girl is having sex with me. They're always having sex with some sort of imaginary person."

"An imaginary person who lives in your body."

Well," Kenny said, "it's not the same thing."

The conversation that ensued was just like the conversations in high school where they picked up on one tiny topic and talked it into the ground.

For Amanda, Kenny has always been like a brother. They talked about sex in an extremely open and blunt manner but it was just too incestuous to think of having sex with each other.

Now he told her about the party that he and his band had last night after the show was over. They were the party – KY Jam, the three band members, and a group of screaming girls. "I was sucked and gnawed at until I was raw."

He shook his head, "The funny thing, you know all those teenage girls I wanted when I was a teenage boy and they wouldn't give me the time of day? They'd do me in the middle of the street now and they would tell the world. I'd be the star of their Facebook page."

Amanda said, "Once again, I'd really like to know what you would like? If you don't want to have sex with adoring screaming fans, who do you want to have sex with?"

"I'd like to have sex with a real woman who was interested in Kenny not in some asshole that I pretend to be."

Curvy Girls

"You mean that you looking to get involved with some nice old-fashioned woman, fall in love, settle down, have kids."

"I don't think so. I don't know." Kenny grinned. "That's the problem. I mainly work all the time. Like we have about 300 gigs a year. There is no such thing as a normal life. I don't think I'd enjoy it anyway. Most of the time, I love my life."

"I like being on the road. Most of the time it's just like the life I imagined." Kenny frowned "It's kind of selfish of me, but it's perfect except that I'd really like to have real sex once in a while not some screaming fan sucking my dick."

Amanda said, "You mean like a regular girlfriend who just, umm, sat around waiting for you?"

Kenny laughed. "Even I know that wouldn't work. Maybe it's just like I wish I had a fuck-buddy or something like that that I need."

Amanda said, "You'd be surprised if I told you what I do for sex."

Kenny opened his eyes wide surprise, "Don't tell me you're a lesbian?" He looked around the apartment. "Clearly you live here with another woman."

Amanda said, "Oh, come on Kenny. How could you be so narrow minded? Just because I have a female roommate who have a seriously really good friendship with, that doesn't mean I'm a lesbian. And if I were, what difference would it make?"

"It wouldn't make much sense except that it would mean you changed a lot since high school."

Kenny was right. Most of the time they spent talking about their lives and dreams and wishes. When it wasn't about those things, it was about Kenny's horniness and his inability to score with the girls or Amanda's horniness and what she'd like to do to one particular football player and his name brand clothes.

Amanda said, "My roommate Amy, our friend Beth and I have a kind of informal club. We call ourselves the Curvy Girls."

She got up and opened the desk drawer. "Just a minute, I will show you." She dug around until she found the ad they had placed when they started their very satisfying sex life.

Amanda explained how she and Amy had advertised for the first members of their sex club. They wanted to get the word out to like-minded people knowing that once they did, word-of-mouth would keep it going.

The men had to be respectful, healthy, well equipped, and willing to play without wanting or expecting commitment.

It worked really well. Most of the guys were wonderful and a genuine affection had developed among the players.

"We get our needs met and it fits our lifestyle. Sometimes we barely have an hour a week to play but we make it work."

"It works great – if I can only show up for an hour, I have an hour's worth of fun. No fuss, no need to do small talk." Amanda grinned, "Now this week, I am done with school and I'm taking life easy for a little while. So I could party every day."

She continued explaining, "There's usually party once a week at Beth's. If I was interested in a little one-on-one, I could call up or text any one of the guys and see what availability he had."

She waved her hand around the apartment and said, "He'd just pop in here. If I want to get laid six times today, I could."

Kenny was intrigued and asked more questions about the curvy girls. Then he asked, "Could I be one of those men in your stable of studs?"

Amanda looked at him seriously, "I was just thinking about that. It's would be weird because – well you know you're like a brother to me so you could go to one of the parties at Beth's but I wouldn't be part of that party. If you still happen to be in town I think she's having one Friday night."

Before Kenny could answer, Amanda said, "I can think of a way around it. It wouldn't really work for you because you are on the road so much but I have an idea forming in my head right now. No big party planned after your show tonight?"

"There usually is. We can't just come off stage and then brush our teeth and go to bed. A guy needs to unwind." Kenny stretched. "It feels good to just be me. Just like old times."

Amanda's Solution

It took a little planning but Amanda came up with a solution. An impromptu party for the guys with girls who were real girls, not screaming groupies. Good basic sensible women who were interested in fun sex.

After the show, Kenny and his friends were to change into ordinary clothes, wash off their makeup and take a cab to Beth's house. They would show up as regular guys ready to party and the clever curvy girls would arrange to have four regular girls meet them at Beth's.

Ever since Amanda had graduated, she knew that she might be moving out of the city. Meanwhile, she and Beth and Amy had discussed the healthy sexual experiences that they had been having with some women they knew who might be interested.

They want to spread the word to a lot of the women they knew. They had already all talked to acquaintances and casual friends about their personal lives.

A couple of them had already been involved in some of the parties and a few ladies since set up a similar type of club amongst themselves. It's a fine line keeping it all fun and exciting without having it become too chaotic.

The whole point of the Curvy Girls was to make having great sex simple and easy. There was no need to set it up as a big elaborate chore of organizing venues and participants.

After brief text conversations with Beth and Amy, Amanda had come up with four women who were interested in being part of the daring experiment in sex. The four women were interested but also somewhat inhibited by their lack of natural sexuality and sensuality. They would be perfect for this party.

Amanda would be the host and would get them all together at Beth's and she laughed as she said to Amy, "I may have to get out the flip chart and explain to them what they are supposed to do."

The Curvy Girls had described to these women that sensuality came from inside, it came from the heart and the brain. It had nothing to do with proper makeup and finely tuned bodies.

Everyone was beautiful if only they allowed it to shine through their shyness, their insecurity, and their fear.

The Women

Irene was a chunky girl who was in her first year of graduate studies. She had beautiful eyes and a sprinkling of freckles across her nose. Her hair was usually tousled and she often controlled by pulling it back in a ponytail.

She seemed to live in no-name jeans that were baggy and long tailed plaid shirts with the sleeves rolled up. She'd worked on a project that Amanda had been involved in and they got to know each other a little bit.

Amanda knew that Irene was horny. Amanda also knew that Irene had no idea how to go about getting laid. She dressed the way she did because she felt that she was ugly. This is what she told Amanda.

Once upon a time, after they finished a project, Amanda had told Irene just little bit about their party's. Amanda called up Irene and she was blunt. She asked if Irene would be interested in going to a party that involved some discreet and no fuss sex.

"I know it's short notice," Amanda said, "but an old friend of mine is in the entertainment field and they're doing a show and they are only here for a few days."

It was easier than Amanda expected. Irene was extremely excited at the idea.

Irene was talking a mile a minute. "My roommate and I were actually thinking about maybe asking you how to get started in something like this."

The natural thing to do was to suggest to Irene that she bring her roommate along. Beth meanwhile said that there was a secretary in her office that she really liked who had been in a bad relationship. Her self-esteem was in the toilet because her boyfriend told her how ugly she was all the time.

Amy had a friend, a colleague in her department who was extremely shy but who had confessed to a horniness that never seemed to leave her. She hadn't had sex in five years and she often feared that she would never have sex again.

So that evening Irene and her roommate, Carla, the secretary from Beth's office, Peggy, and Michaela of Amy's department met at Beth's.

Michaela was the most outspoken one of the group of new women in the Curvy Girls gang. And she was definitely a curvy girl, being well endowed with enormous breasts and very wide hips.

She asked, "When will the guys be here? And what if we find them ugly?"

Irene said, "We shouldn't even think about them being ugly. We all have beauty. What if they are thinking the same thing – maybe we're ugly."

The discussion got lively as the four newcomers who were just getting to know each other discussed the problems with judging people based on their looks.

Finally Amy said, "Have you ever heard of KY Jam?"

Carla shrieked, "Oh my God KY Jam. I love KY Jam. You mean to say that one of them looks like KY Jam? I call dibs on that one."

"I love the drummer, Zeke." Michaela said.

Irene said, "I've heard of them but I don't know what any of them look like."

Peggy took out her phone and flipped through until she found a picture of KY and his band. She showed the picture to Irene.

"It's them," Amanda said.

Peggy looked toward the door, "I didn't hear anybody at the door."

There was some confusion as they all spoke at once expressing nervousness and excitement.

Beth said, "No they're not here yet."

Amanda said, "No I mean it's them – your playmates for the night are KY Jam and his band."

"What?" Michaela said. "Are you serious?"

The other women echoed her sentiments.

Irene asked, "Why didn't you tell us earlier? I would have – dressed better." She was wearing her baggy jeans but she was wearing a nice t-shirt instead of an old plaid shirt.

Michaela said, "Will the drummer be here?"

Amanda explained how she had grown up with Kenny, a.k.a. KY Jam. And how they want a regular sex, not groupie sex.

She and her friends had reached out to these women because they knew that they were horny and they also knew they were smart and sensible and they didn't expect groupie-like behavior from them.

Jam Session

When the boys arrived, they were dressed in street clothes. The point was to make them look a little less overwhelming when they appeared. At the time when she planned this party, Amanda didn't know whether the new party women would be freaked out by rock stars.

Beth had gone to her friend Armand's place for the night. Amy wanted to be there to help the new people get acquainted. "And you never know, one of the girls might back out."

Amanda and Amy made the introductions. Irene was surprised to find herself starstruck. All day she was torn between wishes that she had more advance notice of this party and being glad that she didn't.

Now she knew that if she had known the guys were famous rock stars, she knew for sure that she would not be there.

She and Carla had fantasized about something just like this ever since Irene first heard about the Curvy Girls.

She had sex before but it was not satisfactory. It was limited to groping in the backseat of a car and that was the best of it.

She had also had a brief crush on a fellow student but he was inexperienced and clearly not interested in her just interested in her availability to help him with his research papers.

Irene has never been in a long-term relationship and she liked it that way. She was busy and loved her work and she considered herself a bit of an expert in masturbation.

Michaela and Peggy were quiet. So were the four men. Amanda felt like chaperone. She remembered the first time that the Curvy Girls got together. Beth had the mood lighting and the mood music.

Amanda asked one of the guys to dance and Beth took one of the guys into her bedroom and after that it just unfolded naturally and easily.

She wondered if she should suggest they turn on the music and dance. Or maybe she should encourage one of them to simply reach for someone else's hand and they disappear into one of the bedrooms.

There were two bedrooms on the main floor and two bedrooms upstairs. There was also a Jacuzzi and a music room.

And here these eight people sat and Amanda had a strange feeling that if somebody didn't start something they would all be sitting here when the sun rose in the morning.

The drummer. A short stocky man named Zeke, the drummer, was sitting next to Irene but Amanda noticed that he was looking over at Michaela who was avoiding eye contact.

Michaela said she liked the drummer. So why was she avoiding eye contact?

Amanda consoled herself with the amused thought that this was a lot different from having the groupies crowd in backstage after the show, eager to do whatever the musicians wanted them to do.

Amy finally spoke. She said, "If you really not sure how to get the ball rolling, normally I suggest music but that might be not the best idea. Music for musicians? Not a good idea."

Amanda knew she was babbling but she wanted to get the show on the road. Amanda stood up and said, "Why don't I give a couple of you a tiny tour of the house."

She took Michaela's hand and waved to Zeke. "Come on, Zeke. She guided them to the nearest downstairs bedroom. It had a large bed and two cozy barrel chairs.

Amanda indicated the chairs and said, "Tour's over. Why don't you two get to know each other?"

This is going to be painful, she thought, but when she went back into the living room there was only Amy left in the room. She laughed.

"I'm wiped out. Amy, did they go home?" Amanda asked.

Amy responded with laughter as well, "I was afraid they might. But they seemed to take the hint. Irene snagged Jimbo and then Carla grabbed Kenny's hand."

Down and Dirty

In the bedroom she had chosen upstairs, Irene took matters into her own hands. She was with Jimbo, the wiry guitarist, his pale brown haired seemed electrified, standing out from his head like a halo.

He was sinewy with long bony arms and long bony fingers. He was sitting on the side of the bed. Just sitting. Irene looked at him and wondered if he was so used to women throwing himself at him that he expected her to do all the work and let him lie back and enjoy the process.

Well, Irene thought, I am not some starry eyed little groupie. She removed her clothes one item at a time and let them drop to the floor. She stepped out of her white cotton panties while he watched. He didn't move.

"Now it's your turn," Irene said.

Jimbo had watched her undress and he was surprised by the thick thatch of dark pubic hair and her sturdy broad hips and her enormous tits.

He stood up and undressed the same way that she did, slowly and deliberately letting his clothes drop to the floor.

Irene moved closer to him and he reached for her and pulled her toward him feeling the warmth of her breasts against his rib cage. He ran his hands down her back, along her spine and then over the curve of her hips.

She felt strong and sturdy and smooth. Her skin was like velvet. There were no knobby little bones. Zeke himself was nothing but knobby bones.

He knelt down in front of her, his face at breast level and he took one of her breasts and lifted it. Her nipple was hard and jutted out like the first joint of his little finger.

He took the hard nipple in his mouth and he sucked pressing his teeth against the flesh. Not biting, just feeling her nipple against his teeth. He flicked the end of his tongue against the tip of her nipple.

He moved his hands so he had both breasts captured in them. He moved his head so that he could now pay attention to the other nipple.

Jimbo had always been a tit man. He was in heaven. Jimbo didn't want to take his hands off her enormous jugs.

He guided her to the bed and helped her into a position where he could kneel between her sturdy thighs and buried his face in her boobs. He kissed and nibbled and licked.

He stopped for a moment and looked at her, "I hope you don't mind but I love your tits."

Irene had never had sex with the lights on before. And she had never had anyone focus so intensely only on her breasts.

She said, "I like it." She was on her back and she could feel the heat of his cock pressing against her belly and she felt an urgent tugging inside her. She wanted that cock inside she wanted to be fucked and fucked hard.

She wanted him to play with her tits. Oh the exquisite joy of being touched and licked and fondled. Her entire body was tingling with the touch and the anticipation.

Jimbo continued to fondle her tits, sucking and squeezing. Irene began thrusting her hips up toward him and moaning. He could feel his pre-cum oozing onto her belly and he moved one hand down between her thighs.

Between her legs he felt that thatch of pubic hair. He had seen pussies like that in some of the older porn movies that he entertained himself with all during teen years.

In real life, he had never felt a fistful of pubic hair like this. He had never even seen one in real life. He wiggled his fingers through the nest of her hair and found her lips and parted them.

She was damp. He reached for his cock and he guided it to the dampness and then he slowly let it slide into her as she pressed her hips upward to accept his cock.

He wrapped his arms around her tits, put his lips on her forehead and began rocking rhythmically in and out.

In the next room, Kenny and Carla were lying naked facing each other. Carla's hand was resting on his waist and he had a hand on her hip.

Kenny was savoring the tranquility of the moment. He had the music in his head and he could feel the lights flashing, and the sounds of poetry without words. This is a real woman. He ran his hand over her hip cupping her ass while he brought his other hand around to her front.

He ran his fingers over her pussy, feeling the crack of her pussy lips were pressed together. He ran his fingers lightly along the pussy seam and up to the top where he could feel her hard little knob.

As he played along this warm and silky area he kept staring into her eyes. They were a remarkable violet color. She wasn't wearing lipstick.

He placed lips against hers and savored the non-greasy, non-waxy taste of her lips. She smelled like mint.

Kenny moved his mouth down to her tiny tits. They were hardly mounds at all. They were just huge nipples with swollen aureoles and hard but tiny nubs. He sucked them one at a time.

He could feel the dampness on his hand was still between her legs.

"Do you want me to fuck you?" He whispered.

"Yes."

He guided her to her back and then to her other side so that she was spooned against him, her copious ass pressed up against his erection.

He reached down and ran his hand between the cheeks of her ass lifting and separating them so that he could put his cock between her legs. He let his cock explore her nether regions until the tip of it reached her sweet dampness.

Carla arched her back and he could feel her ass pressing up against his lower belly and his upper thighs as he slid his turgid hardon into her.

He pulled his cock out as far as he could, keeping just the head of it at her entrance and then slammed it back into her as hard as he could. She moaned.

He pulled it out slowly and thrusted hard back into her. Again and again. His arms were around her and his fingers were busy manipulating her clitoris while he fucked her from behind.

Pinching her nipples gently, Kenny loved the feel of her body against him, warm and solid and responsive. He didn't want this fucking to end. Not just yet.

Greg played bass. Now he was strumming his fingers along Peggy's body. He liked groupies because they were always willing and eager to give him a blow job without any need for conversational foreplay.

He really didn't know what to say to Peggy or even if he needed to talk to her. He had smoked a great big doobie on the way over and he was floating. This is a whole new experience for him, stretched out in a big bed with big soft woman beside him.

He didn't want to move, he just want to let his fingers feel the music in her body. As he drifted deeper and deeper into the sensations he could feel his cock finally stir.

He was lying on his side and Carla was on her back. His left hand propped his head up while his right hand moved over her soft belly and between her legs. It kept moving up and down reaching her breasts and then moving back to her pussy.

His eyes were closed and he had a beatific smile on his face. When his cock began to stir it was pressing against Peggy's hip. She closed her hand over his cock and squeezed. He moved his hips back and forth slightly as if he were fucking her cupped hand.

He could feel her heat and he realized that in spite of all the times he had his cock sucked just this year, it had been ages since he had savored the sweet taste of pussy juice.

He opened his eyes and looked at Peggy. Then he smiled. "There something I got to do," he said. And he shifted himself into position with his head between her thighs.

"I got a get me some of this pussy." He darted his tongue at her clit and then ran along the seam of her pussy lips. Then he burrowed in, licking and lapping along the length of her vagina's opening.

Taking her clit between his lips, he stretched his arms up along her sides and stroked her rib cage, her waist and over her hips. Greg reveled in her luxurious body.

Carla was riding herself to her fourth orgasm on Zeke's thick and turgid cock. It was a curved penis which, if she sat straight up on him, had the tip of his penis directly hitting on her G spot. She took short strokes, she took long strokes, she moved until she felt the tingle and gush of her G spot and stopped, holding herself in that exquisite position.

She knew she would never get enough of this so she wanted to take as much as she could right now.

The Morning After

Amanda and Amy had gone home after the partiers were all paired off. Beth had no intention of coming home, she planned to go straight to work from Armand's place.

When Amanda let herself in, the house was eerily silent except for the loud snores coming from one of the room.

Amanda had brought the basic makings of breakfast with her. She put on a pot of coffee and put the container of orange juice in the fridge.

She drank the coffee and read her book and no one disturbed her until midmorning. One by one, people began appearing. She was grateful that Kenny was wearing jeans. Two of the other guys were wearing nothing but smiles.

Each bedroom had capacious cotton robes hanging on hooks behind the door and all four women were wearing these robes.

Everyone looked disheveled. Amanda made a fresh pot of coffee, Greg poured himself one and now he was standing on the deck, coffee in one hand and a hand rolled cigarette in the other.

The group was almost as quiet as they had been the night before but there was none of the strange tension in the air.

It was a quiet of well rested and well fucked people who had nothing to worry about at that very moment.

Zeke and Jimbo joined Greg on the deck and soon Kenny went out to be with them.

They were all going through the motions of playing their invisible instruments and working on riffs.

Irene spoke first, "I think music is their passion."

Carla agreed, nodding her head. Peggy said, "I think couple of them have other passions too." She smiled.

Michaela agreed with her. "Oh yes."

Irene said, "That was an incredible experience. This is the kind of stuff that you Curvy Girls do all the time?"

Amanda said, "Kind of. It's a little different. Most of the time they are not rock stars."

Peggy said, "Beth mentioned that you get together and have some sort of interesting parties but she never said how often you do."

Amanda explained that none of it was too regimented. There was no set schedule with behaviors that were repeated. It was just a group of horny people who put the real focus of their life elsewhere.

"But every now and then we just need a really good piece of tail."

KY Jam Moves On

Kenny called Amanda before he and his band moved on to the next gig.

He wanted to get together again but he was scheduled to be on a late-night talk show and they had to be on the go early in the morning.

"I just wanted to thank you for last night. That was a lot of fun. That's what I kind of thought college would be like – if I'd gone to college."

"Kenny," Amanda said, "do you have any idea who you are?"

"You mean the self-knowledge thing?" He and Amanda had spent a lot of their adolescent years discussing the meaning of life and their role in the universe.

"You goof." Amanda laugh, "I mean who KY Jam is?"

"To me KY Jam is just a goofy name that I made up. I mean when I heard about KY jelly the name just came to me."

Amanda said, "I mean who the character is, what a rock star is?"

Kenny side, "I know what it is to me Mandy, it's an invention. I think that's why I had such a good time last night. I mean, it was like real people having a real sex." He paused and added, "She looked me in the eye. She saw that I was a real person."

"I'm glad Kenny," Amanda said.

"She gave me her phone number and her email address."

"Will you use it?"

"I'd like to," Kenny said. "But work really gets in the way. By the time I get back this way, she'll likely be married have kids."

The New Curvy Girls

Irene, Carla, Michaela, and Peggy got together just for them to talk about their night with the rock stars. They played YouTube videos of KY Jam and the band and shared memories of their escapade.

Then Michaela said, "Come on girls, let's get real about this. That was a lot of fun with those guys. But we got to be careful. We don't want to do what women like us always do, get caught up in the romance and glamour and we let life pass us by."

She looked at all of them intensely and continued, "We got to have a lot more fun. Let's do what Amy and Amanda do."

"And Beth. Don't forget Beth," said Peggy.

And so, they began planning their next party.

Curvy Girls Do It Wetter and Steamy

Irene and Carla

Irene looked at her naked body in the full length mirror in her bedroom. She had rarely spent much time reviewing her attributes. If you had asked her what she looked like, she would not have been able to give you a very detailed answer.

Her skin was white, pale with blue tinges. Her breasts were pendulous, drooping slightly but they had to droop. It was a simple law of gravity.

It wasn't that they were saggy just that they were big. Not the puffed up grandeur of silicon tits that looked like beach balls had been inserted under the skin of the stars of porn magazines.

Her nipples were long when they were hard and flat when they were soft. They were a pale pink against her white skin.

She patted her belly. It was big but still firm. She had no real waist indentation at all but with her big tits and wide hips, she did have a bit of a girly shape.

Her legs were good. Muscular and sturdy and her ankles were slender enough to give her a shapely leg. It was just a bigger shape than the typical size two girl.

Irene was a very smart woman. She always thought of herself as having brains but not beauty. And she was okay with that. She was a well endowed woman and she had all the desires of a woman.

Actually she had such strong desires that It wasn't easy for her trying to concentrate sometimes when her desires got the best of her.

Ever since she had her first encounter with sex just for the sake of sex, Irene had a new outlook on life. Rather than pine away wishing for a partner who could satisfy her needs, she knew that there was another way to get all the sex she needed and she didn't have to worry about the guy losing interest or failing to have her level of horniness.

She took a look at her wardrobe. Shape jeans. A collection of men's shirts she liked because they covered her figure. Plain white cotton undies because they were supposed to be healthy. Industrial sized bras.

She needed to think about replacing some of her ratty old panties and worn out bras. She could look into finding something that was not quite so utilitarian.

Well she wasn't about to become all girly. That wasn't who she was. But now that she had new insight into the possibilities of expanding her sexual experience, things could change.

One night with a rock star had made her acutely aware of her body and the pleasures it could bring. She could not stop thinking about it.

She was aware that the day after her night of passion made her feel smarter. Her mind was clear. She was on top of everything that day. It could've been as simple as being out of the office and away from her daily pressures.

A change is as good as a rest, as the old saying put it.

Or it could've been the multiple orgasms that pleased her and set off hormones she had not felt before. Even if she was smarter, it didn't matter. The important thing was that she had fun.

She could see the difference in her roommate Carla's approach to life as well. Carla was very shy woman, with low self-esteem. She didn't like her body, and she didn't think she was worth anything.

That was the way that Carla had been as long as Irene knew her. But ever since the night with the rock stars, Carla was beginning to wonder if maybe there was something good about herself after all.

This was an old conversation they had had many times. Carla would say things like, "I'm the ugly girl that the pretty girls like to hang around with because it makes them look even prettier."

"What? What do you mean?" Irene would ask.

"You know what I mean," Carla would say. "I'm ugly."

Irene always snapped at her. "I've heard that before and it always continued to add that the so-called ugly girls were hanging around the pretty girls because they get the leftovers."

Carla flared up at that. "Leftovers! Leftovers."

"Well, if you take your thinking through the logical next step, that's what it is," Irene said. If nothing else Irene was very practical person. She saw logic everywhere and if she didn't see logic, she created it.

Since the night with the rock stars, Carla was less critical of herself.

They had been in touch with Michaela and Peggy who had been with them that night. It had created a bit of a bond among them.

But their lives were all going in different directions. Irene for instance was getting ready to graduate. It was her undergraduate degree and she felt that it was going to open doors for her. She just had no personal plans for the future yet.

Carla was always making plans for her future where she would be successful and rich. Irene speculated that it was just Carla's way to build up her sense of self esteem.

Carla was a remarkable person. If only she knew it.

Just Talking

Okay," Carla said, "tell me what you do." They were sitting in the living room, watching a rerun on television.

"Do about what?"

Carla continued, "About having a situation like your friend there have. Amanda and her buddies with the sex."

Irene was silent. Not because she didn't want to answer but because she didn't yet have an answer.

"I suppose, I could ask Amanda if they have any leftovers."

Carla shook her head, "You and your leftovers." She had been hurt by the accuracy of how Irene described Carla's life, willing to accept the leftovers from the table of her prettier friends.

In high school she had hung out with a couple of friends who were quite attractive and spent a great deal of time fixing their make up and choosing just the right clothes. They were nice, pleasant girls and they were kind to Carla.

But she always did end up with the guys who really want to be with somebody else.

Irene said, "Well if you have a better idea, let me hear it."

Carla said "You know part of the excitement of the other night was being in that house. There was just something otherworldly about it. I mean what if we had to invite the guys back here."

She indicated the apartment. It was a spacious apartment, the top half of an old Victorian mansion. But it was decorated in early student.

It even had brick and plank bookshelves. And it was messy. They were papers, clothes, books, and assorted grocery bags full of everything but groceries all over the place.

"Well," Irene said, "I suppose we could start by tidying up a bit."

Carla said, "I got a better idea. Why don't we hire one of those companies, you know, that will send a couple of people in here who will clean it right up."

Irene said, "Sure. Why not? I can take in my pizza and beer budget for the week and that should pay for my share of the cost."

Silently, she thought it might also be a healthy choice to forgo pizza and beer once in a while. Not, she reminded herself, that she wanted to or even needed to lose weight.

So that was the first step. They called the Campus Maid Service. Which really wasn't related to the campus at all other than it catered to members of the campus.

Irene didn't like the name. She thought it was false advertising.

Carla said, "Oh for heavens sake, Irene, give it a rest. They often hire students to work with them so that gives a bit of credibility as a campus institution."

A Clean House, A Dirty Mind

The apartment sparkled when the girls came home from class after the cleaners had been there. It even had a certain type of elegance. It also smelled good.

Well, Irene thought, the first step is taken. Now all we do is find the guys to play with.

Irene had a moment's concern with the notion of finding men. But that was part of her nature. Everything in Irene's life had to be analyzed and calculated and measured.

She was all too familiar with the exhortation to find your fears and face them.

This of course sent her off into another direction of analysis. What were her fears? She realized that she had the double set of fears.

She had fears of never having a sex life. And she had fears of men. She had been hurt by men. Now she realized that was not accurate. She had been hurt by boys. Not men. Boys. Silly high school stuff.

She was all too aware that for a lot of teenage boys women were just life support systems for tits.

She had gone out on a few dates with a classmate and once he got his hands on her tits not on her pussy, he said things that hurt her.

He said, "Come on Irene. Get real. If you ever want to get asked out on a date, you are going to have to learn to put out."

It was cruel and heartless especially coming from someone that she thought actually liked her.

She had begged her parents for breast reduction surgery but they wouldn't permit it and her mother, a strong feminist, scolded her about wanting to alter her perfect body in any way, shape, or form.

Her mother insisted that this was the body nature gave her and she had no right at all to want to change it. Her mother was so adamant about being a natural woman that the notion of plucking her eyebrows had caused her some concern.

Irene took a bubble bath and luxuriated in the incense aroma and their sparkling bathroom. Motivated by how good it felt to live in a clean place, Irene was diligent about dealing with the damp towels and face clothes and the bottles and tubes she had used during her bath.

She wiped out the bathtub too which showed traces of the whiskers following her diligent leg shaving and armpit shaving.

It was something that she had done over the years but only when the mood struck. She wasn't too bad today because she had given itself a few licks with the razor before meeting the rock stars.

But it didn't take long for the bristles to return.

Let The Games Begin

Carla came home from classes the next day all excited. "I think I met couple of guys who might be willing to play."

Irene inwardly rolled her eyes but she turned a smiling face to Carla. Irene could see it now, a couple of horny undergraduates who knew even less about sex than they did.

She said to Carla, "So who do you have in mind?"

"One of the guy who teaches one of my labs. Scott. He is graduate student, I think, in biology."

"What do you mean, you think in biology? Is it a biology lab he teaches?"

"I mean I think he's a graduate student. I know he's in biology."

Irene nodded, "Go on."

"Well, he's always been really easy to talk to but I never thought of him as a kind of um, uh, what would I say...as the kind of guy I would date."

Ah. Irene thought, there must be something really wrong with him if Carla never would have thought of dating them.

"Why wouldn't you date him?"

"I don't know really. I mean, he's not bad looking. He's not too tall, not too short. Not too fat, not too thin. I just never really felt any kind of spark with him."

Irene said, "Okay, so I suppose he could be one."

"Well, he's got a friend."

Irene had a thought and she felt that she had to ask it because she was the kind of person who always think things all the way through.

So she asked, "You don't suppose he and his friend are in a relationship with each other, do you?"

"Oh come on Irene, how stupid do you think I am? No he's got a friend and I asked him, you know we were just talking, about graduate school –."

"So then you must know he was in graduate school..."

"No I don't. But I had to find a way to start the conversation. He never said that he was. We were just talking about school and how hard it is to have a personal life."

Carla said, somewhat crankily, "Irene, it doesn't matter. The point is, I talked to him about sex."

"I told him how you and I talked about how we like to have sex but didn't need all the bullshit that went with it."

Irene stared at her. Would she never get to the point?

"And?" Irene prompted.

"Well, the bottom line is he thought it was a funny conversation to have in the lab."

Irene held her tongue. There was nothing she could do but let Carla go on and tell the story in her own way. Even though Irene was itching to shake the words out of Carla.

"He said he and his buddy used to go out to the bars and try to pick up girls. But he said it doesn't work. It's kind of like, I think, false advertising. At least that's what I said and he said that is exactly the way it was."

"The problem they would try to pick up a couple of girls to have sex with. But it never felt quite right because he always felt girls were out there looking for more than just sex."

Carla could see Irene was about to hop on her feminist hobbyhorse so she kept on talking, "We talked about that and I told him I knew what he was talking about. I said sometimes I just want to get together with some guy and have a good time."

Carla hardly drew a breath. She just kept on spilling out the words. "But if I ever suggested that to a guy, I knew he would get all confused and start thinking that I was acting like I was interested in a relationship with him."

Carla stopped. She didn't like talking about this now. The reality was that there was a time when she was interested in a relationship.

She always thought that unless she had a boyfriend there was something wrong with her. And there was. She was also afraid that just because she wasn't the typical size, she might be willing to settle for anything.

It was a complicated area and Carla had long ago decided not to spend a lot of time wallowing in analyzing what life was all about.

Unlike Irene who had to analyze everything. Like now, she was sure that Irene was going to come up with all kinds of protestations.

Irene surprised her and asked, "So, did you set up a date?"

"Not really. I told him I had to check and see if you were available.

Irene did not want to be interrupting all the time, so she nodded and waved a hand in a "go on" signal.

"Well they're available Friday night, if you are." Carla said.

Irene was. As also as an afterthought she asked, "Do you have any idea what his friend looks like?"

"Not a clue." Carla said.

Meeting the Guys

Paul drove the car and Scott gave directions. They were very quiet on the way to meet Irene and Carla. Paul put the car in park and turned off the engine.

Then he put his hands on the steering and leaned forward, dropping his head to the steering wheel.

"I must be out of my mind to go along with this. I mean, how whacky are these broads anyway?" Paul moaned.

Scott said, "Whacky enough that you better not call them broads to their faces."

"Scott, you got to tell me the truth. They're not real dogs, are they?"

Paul said, "I never met Irene. But Carla. I like her. She's smart, and real nice."

"Code words. Smart. Nice." Paul looked at his buddy and said, "Oh my God, these must be real dogs."

Scott said, "Come on, Paul. It's as if we score with the hot girls. Really. How many times have we been able to make it with really pretty girls."

"And I happen to think Carla's quite cute."

"Well if she's so cute, what's she doing, hitting on you? Inviting us to their place for wild and crazy sex?"

Scott said, "It wasn't exactly like that. She and I just got talking about how sometimes a person just wants to get laid. And how so many people make it such a big deal. Like you're doing right now."

Paul said, "Okay. Okay, I'm going with you but we got to have some sort of escape word."

"Escape word?"

"You know something we say. A good signal in case one of us just has to get out of there."

Scott said, "Okay. Riverboat. If either of us want to get the hell out of there. We just simply say riverboat."

All nonchalant. Scott rang the doorbell. The buzzer rang, the door clicked and they were on their way up the stairs.

Paul was ready to expect the worst. He was pleasantly surprised that both women were actually pretty decent looking. They were chubby but pleasant to look at.

Irene's hair was better than very nice. It was really long and silky. It flowed over her shoulders and down her back almost to her big round ass.

There were candles flickering around the room placed strategically off to the edges of the big living room. In the background he could hear low music playing.

It was really low and he was not sure what was playing but it sounded like rock music. He wasn't into rock but played really low like this, it was appealing.

The girls had laid out a tray of crackers and cheese on the big square coffee table. The table was surrounded by a loveseat and three arm chairs.

Irene offered the boys herbal tea or coffee or water. It had a strange kind of feeling like any time one of the parents would pop out and demand to know what their intentions really were.

He and Scott sat in the chair and they were all rather shy with each other. Paul continued to look over the girls as discreetly as he could.

They were both very big-assed women. Irene had a square bill, broad hips, big boobs and thick waist. Carla was very broad in the rear but her waist was nipped in.

Her tits were tiny. He could see that and her shoulders were wide. She had a broad face with what his mother would call Slavic cheek bones.

Her hair was short and blonde and very curly, almost kinky it was so curly.

Carla was talking to Scott. The next thing Scott knew, Carla said, "Well, come with me. I want to show you my etchings."

Scott got up and followed her to the door on the left side of the living room.

Paul looked at Irene and frowned, "Etchings?"

"Carla's idea of humor. It's something she picked up some old movie, I think. Or something she read where the wicked seducer lures innocent young women in his home on the pretext of showing them his art."

Paul looked at her directly in the eyes and asked, "Do you have any etchings?"

Irene said, "I don't know. Let's go and see."

She started to walk toward her bedroom on the right side of the living room. She stopped at the door and turned to look at Paul, who was still sitting in the chair.

"Come on," she said. "I'm not going to bite you." She laughed and added, whimsically for her, "Unless you want me to."

Paul was not quite as tall as Irene. And he was a little chunky too, he had to admit. He figured that the two of them probably weighed about the same.

For a brief moment he wondered if she thought he was a dog. The idea almost immediately deflated his pecker.

He had not had sex in six months and that had not been all that satisfying. The girl was drunk and so, as a matter of fact, was he.

It'd been some party on campus and she had started talking to him and the more they talked, the more beer they had. The more beer they had the prettier she looked and the more handsome he looked.

Paul had another moment of starting truth, when he realized that he was so grateful that this pretty girl at the party was talking to him that he could've fallen in love with her just because she paid attention to him.

That's why he had been still sitting and staring at Irene who was in the doorway to her bedroom.

What a lousy time to have a crisis of self-esteem. He felt awkward and ugly and now he was terrified that his cock would stand up to the occasion.

Well, even if his cock would stand up, he would.

He got up and walked toward her. He hoped she could not hear his heart thumping. He was both nervous and excited.

She held out a hand to one of his and guided him into her bedroom. It was the big room with a very high ceiling and very tall windows.

Irene turned to him and asked, "Do you mind if I start slow?"

Paul shook his head, no. The room was dimly lit and he wasn't sure that she could see him shake his head, and so he added, "Not at all. I'd love to start slow."

Irene stretched out on top of the duvet that covered her bed. He lay down beside her. She rolled over so that she was facing him directly.

They looked into each other's eyes.

"You have remarkable hair," Paul said.

Irene looked at his hairline, which was already receding, and Paul immediately regretted having mentioned hair at all. His hair was nondescript and there was less of it every year.

Carla Gets It On

Scott said, "I can't believe what we're doing." He was naked and cock was thrumming, it was so hard.

It had been months he had had sex and to relieve his excitement, he had pulled himself that morning. He noticed that after a while masturbation seems to have the reverse effect to what it is supposed.

Yanking himself only made him hornier.

Carla's body stripped of all her clothes was like a painting. It had more shape than her clothing revealed. Carla's hips were firm and they were dimpled on either side. His hands wanted to play with her round buttocks.

Scott reached out with his two hands and pulled her closer to him. They were standing and his cock was sticking straight out. It pressed up against her stomach as she walked into his embrace.

He placed his lips on her mouth and was surprised at the warm of her lips. He probed her mouth with his tongue and she probed back. He could feel her hips move in an automatic, involuntary, thrusting manner.

I may not last long," Scott said. There was something so erotic about being naked with this sweet woman. Something erotic in knowing that he was just minutes away from the satisfying long warm wet slide into her vagina.

All that he had to do was walk her to the edge of the bed. She could fall back on the bed and he could part her thighs and press his urgent penis into her warm pussy.

Even thinking about it he could already feel his balls tighten and his hot load gather.

Carla said, "If that happens the good news is we can rest up and start over again."

Scott said, "I think we might have to do that."

Scott guided her to the edge of the bed and then onto her back. As he did so he dropped to his knees and pressed his face between her legs.

He rubbed his lips over her soft pubic mound and then felt her clit. He darted his tongue out and licked it.

She moaned.

Scott had seen lot of pussy licked in the videos he loved to watch. Clean shaven and white lips spread to reveal deep purple swollen labia.

He moved his hands to Carla's vagina and tucked them neatly between her thighs, the palms of his hand cupping her pussy lips.

Then he parted them. She was pale white inside and out. She was like a beautiful flower, with layer upon layer of recesses and hidden folds.

He moved his thumbs to capture her inner opening. Then he moved his hands up and caught her nub of passion between them and he rolled it between his thumbs.

He moved his thumbs back and forth as if he was given her a very tiny hand job. It was as if she had a tiny penis.

She began to moan and he realized that she was coming. He didn't want to change his position because whatever he was doing was working for her.

He continued his manipulation of her snatch. She had her fingers in his hair and was clutching and tugging it. She was pushing her pussy against his hands.

"Ohhhh. Ohhh, that is so good." Then her hands loosened the grasp on his hair. Scott moved up so that his cock was where his thumbs had been.

She was damp. She was wet. She was ready.

Scott felt the head of his cock at the entrance to her slick goal, her willing pussy, and pushed himself into her. He could feel the load moving up from his balls and he knew what was about to happen.

Soon shot after shot after shot of his jism squirted out of him and into her as he penetrated her so deeply. Finally, he was spent. He could come no more, still he did not want to move away from her.

His cock head descended into a temporary rest. It was withdrawing from her cunt all by itself.

Scott lifted her legs onto the bed and turned her around so that she was fully laying on the bed. He climbed over and stretched out beside her.

"I –," he began. But Carla laid a finger on his lips.

"Don't say you're sorry," she said. "Save your energy. We're going to do this again."

Irene's Delight

Irene and Paul slowly moved toward each other and they each unbuttoned and unzipped each other until they were completely naked.

He was surprised how well they fit together. He had been concerned that their bellies might get in the way but the reality was she snuggled into him perfectly.

It was a perfect fit as they snuggled shoulder to shoulder. He wasn't sure where to begin so he went with what he wanted. He wanted to feel the solid ass under him.

In spite of all the fancy actions he had seen in the porn movies, all he wanted right now was to feel his cock inside this big beautiful woman.

He lifted himself up and over her, putting one knee between her thighs. And then the second knee beside it. She spread her legs apart to accommodate him.

This was it. This was so different from any of his previous encounters with pussy. He was sober. His cock was ready and willing. He was facing a woman, sober and naked, his dark curly body hair and her dark curly pubic hair blending together down at their crotches.

He looked down and saw his thick staff's dark root showing where it disappeared into her dark thatch.

She was wet and slick. It was exquisite. It was different.

Irene had had recent experience that gave her more courage than usual. It didn't matter how many lovers Paul had or how many lovers she had.

All that mattered was this moment. Naked. A huge cock sliding in and out and in and out.

She didn't know how to build a stable of studs. She was even sure that this man qualified as a stud. In fact, she wasn't sure what a stud was.

Wouldn't the stud factor be in the eyes of the beholder?

In that case, at this moment in time Paul was her stud. He was putting his weight on his arms holding himself just slightly above her blooming bosoms.

She looked up at him and was about to ask whether she should change her position somehow. Should she wrap her legs around his hips? Should she tell him it was all right to put a little more of his weight on her tits?

She didn't ask. She opted to do something that she realized something entirely new for her. She said nothing. She just smiled at them. He smiled back and thrust a little more vigorously.

Irene soon realized that perhaps this was the only position Paul knew. And she didn't care. It worked for her.

Just as she was feeling that she could handle this rhythm all night long, she realized that he was going to come and come soon.

She felt Paul slow on top of her, and she felt a certain amount of disappointment. She had gotten a taste of sex and it was enticing and enchanting and enervating and energizing.

She wanted more and in a perfect world, she thought she would have someone else step in right now and keep up the rhythm and bring her to her next orgasm. She did not want it to end.

Then she realized she was being unreasonable. She had already had an orgasm or two or three and he was just about to have one. Could she begrudge him that?

Then Irene realized that she didn't care. This was all about her and her enjoyment of sex and her pleasure. It was about the lessons that she could learn.

In any case, he kept on thrusting into her. Occasionally, he would change the angle of the thrust, lifting himself up a little more so his thrusts were higher, rubbing against her clitoris or leaning back a little and thrusting low her.

When you're not used to a lot of sex a good old-fashioned fucking really meets the basic needs. Irene had learned something new about herself and that was that if she held her hips in a certain way she got better contact with his cock where it rubbed into her.

So she moved into that position. Maybe it was the joy of the constant pounding of his dick, but she suddenly realized she was about to have another huge orgasm.

The excitement of knowing that she was going to come again and knowing that he was about to shoot a hot load of semen into her, brought Irene to the edge of her own climax.

And then it took her over the edge of her climax into a dizzying swirling series of orgasms.

Then he came. In spite of being over already, Irene had to admit to herself that sure was better than playing with her own cunt. Paul was still on top of her and she could feel his cock shrink.

He didn't move and soon she felt his cock revive.

"Can you handle some more?" he asked.

"Oh yes," she said.

The Morning After

The boys had not made arrangements for the morning after. Neither had the girls. When they woke up, no one really knew what to do other than to start all over again.

After you have fucked and sucked on and off most of the night, it did not seem so daunting to have to head to the bathroom to ease their full bladders. The jug of water was still on the coffee table and as each person separately took a bathroom break, they each got a glass of water.

And they each returned to the bedrooms. Morning sex can be wonderful and when no one was hung over, it was even more fun.

Scott was the one who offered to make coffee. He debated inviting the girls out for breakfast but he didn't want them to think he was trying to turn this into more than a fuck buddy session.

He remembered the discussion with Carla about just wanting to get laid. He didn't want to get into the dating scene. And clearly neither did she.

By the time the coffee was done brewing, all four of them were back in the living room.

Scott said, "Fantastic idea, ladies. Just fantastic."

Both women smiled. Irene said, "I think so."

Paul said, "I wish it was just starting."

Carla said, "Well we can do it again."

Scott said, half joking but entirely in earnest, "How about tonight?"

The women looked at each other and shrugged their shoulders. "Sure. Why not?"

Paul said, "How about the same time, same place?"

Scott said, "We'll bring pizza."

Carla said, "It's a date." Then she laughed. "Well maybe not a date...but...."

"Quit while you're ahead, Carla," Irene teased.

"See you at eight," Carla said.

Irene and Carla tidied up after the men left and did a recap of the night.

Irene said, "I was surprised that they stayed all night."

"Luckily we found something to do," Carla replied.

They were quiet for a bit and then Irene said, "Should we be careful about not making this too much of a routine?"

"You mean the fuck buddy session or fucking those two guys all the time," Carla asked.

"Fucking those two. I mean, I really like Paul, but the whole point was to not get too involved in a relationship with all the trappings that come with it."

"Let's play it by ear," Carla said. "We can keep our eyes open for more playmates."

"I wonder if I can ever get enough sex," Irene said. She could not get it out of her mind that feeling when she knew Paul was going to come. That feeling that she was no where near ready to have the fucking to stop.

Not then. Not for a long time.

She had expected him to pull it out, roll over, probably fall asleep and then be gone as soon as she fell asleep herself.

"You mean you want more now?" Carla said. "I'm a little sore."

"I am too. I guess it's more like I am afraid to just let go and enjoy it because I never know when the next screwing is going to take place."

Carla said, "You're hopeless. You know there'll be more tonight."

"But what about next week?" Irene laughed. "I get it – we just make sure we have more guys in our stable."

Curvy Girls Do It Collection
9 Complete Erotic Romance Stories
4

She understood now what Amy and Amanda had explained to her about how much fun sex could be if she could learn how to use it to her own advantage.

It was a comforting thought to know that she was finally in charge of her own pleasure. She had more sex in the past couple of weeks than she had in her entire life.

And she was only just beginning.

4

Bonus Content

Curvy Girls Do It at Graduation Party

Once More With Passion

Irene and Carla had started their new quest for the cure for their horniness. The first couple of time with new men had been exciting and fun. They were motivated to try it again.

This time they wanted something a little different. There was a graduation coming up and they knew it would be pretty easy to get invited to a variety of graduation parties.

Irene, always practical, said, "I don't want us to get a reputation for being party girls."

Carla asked, "Why not?"

"Think about it, Carla," Irene said. "The whole point of this new sexual freedom we seek is to get to pick and choose who we fuck. And they better be good at it."

She continued, "We're not going there to one of those grad parties like some competitive little bitches looking to make it with the star football player."

"There's a fine line between a girl having fun and a girl being a complete slut."

Carla said, "I can't believe these thoughts still exist. It's so old-fashioned. This is graduation from university, this is grown-up people having a grown up party. How else are we going to build up a stable of really great fucks to entertain ourselves with?"

Irene nodded. She hated to admit it but Carla was right. It wasn't like they were holding out for dates with these guys. They just wanted to get laid, well laid.

She just hated looking desperate. Well, she wasn't desperate. But just the same, to a bunch of horny frat boys, a couple of fat girls might appear to be too eager to please.

Their first adventure on their own had turned out really really well. The guys were inexperience but they were eager and quite nice. In her case, Irene was really pleased that her fuck buddy for the evening was able to get it up for three separate encounters.

Never mind that the first one was a really short encounter, the second and third really made up for that. She had been chaffed for days from his thick cock probing her pussy.

But they needed a bigger stable of studs. Also, Irene could not forget that momentary thought after Paul had come so quickly on their first fuck session. Irene had started thinking about what it would be like to pull a train.

She had heard that phrase before and always thought it was disgusting. But now sitting here talking to Carla about having some fun at a graduation party, Irene kept thinking about what it would be like to be fucked by a stream of several guys.

She imagined one of them sucking her pussy and two of them each attending to one of her tits and a fourth one waiting to serve her.

Irene loved the idea of being completely smothered in man flesh. She took that thought and tried to shape it so that she could talk to Carla about it.

Frat Boys Delight

This was the idea that Irene eventually came up with. She thought it would be interesting to go to a graduation party at one of the fraternities.

She didn't care whether it was the geeky fraternity where the guys with thick glasses and scraggly hair talked about coding or the jock fraternity where they knew how to party but it seemed to take a lot of them forever to graduate or one of the fraternities where the boys were aloof and snobbish.

She knew enough about fraternities to know that underneath their blazers and their hoodies and their rude T-shirts, the guys were all the same. Horny. Guys.

Her idea was that they would have auditions at the fraternity of their choice. This would give her and Carla control.

All they had to worry about was that the fuck room was a decent place. They did not want a typical fraternity with grungy bedrooms. They also didn't want to show up as a pair of sluts taking on a bunch of different guys on top of the jackets piled on the bed in one of the grungy rooms.

This would put her and Carla in the driver's seat. It depended on the reception they got when they went to the fraternities and told the head committee what they planned.

The auditions were a very simple concept Carla and Irene would set themselves up in a designated room and let it be known that one or the other of them was willing to take on any guy who showed up not drunk and who could produce an adequate hard on.

The first party was filled with business students.

The deal was she and Irene would take turns fucking the applicants for their club. One could tidy up while the other entertained the next contestant.

Irene saw that the waiting list was getting fairly long she felt that the most expedient way to move things along was to ask the host who was the president of the fraternity if they could have access to another bedroom as well.

A second bedroom had been hastily tidied up. They did not want to keep one guy waiting while someone else was using the bed. Irene didn't think that either of them were ready yet for doing it in the same bed.

Maybe if she had been more experienced, she might suggest that She and Carla, side by side, getting royally screwed.

The president was all too willing to accommodate her. She went back into the bedroom where Carla was receiving the turgid attentions of a narrow hipped serious looking young man who had developed a reasonable rhythm and was plowing into her with great speed.

Carla had her legs wrapped around his waist and she seemed to be enjoying herself. Outside the bedroom door where Carla was entertaining, the next guy in line was looking pretty excited. He was tall and slender with narrow shoulders and floppy brown hair. He had an extremely big nose and Irene wondered if this indicated that perhaps he was extremely well-equipped. Well there was no time

like the present, she thought, to check out that old myth.

"Come with me," she said and took his hand and led him to the other bedroom.

She was wearing a simple dress which she pulled over her head then she deftly unhooked her own bra. She was glad that she had replaced her utilitarian cotton bras with more glamorous bras. She stepped out of her matching panties.

He stood there still fully clothed as if he didn't know what to do. Irene got on the bed and said, "Well cutie, are you ready for your audition?"

He quickly pulled his shirt, buttoned though it was, over his head and unbuckled his slacks. He pulled his slacks and his underpants down in one motion and stepped out of his loafers.

He was still wearing black socks but Irene's attention was taken with the gigantic cock on the skinny kid.

"Bring that big boy over here," she said. He stepped toward her and she reached for his swaying dick. His cock was as long and thick as salami.

She reached for it with one hand and wrapped her fingers around it. She was surprised that her fingertips couldn't close, he was that thick.

She raised her knees up and she was lying on her back. She shifted knees so that her feet were flat against the mattress and her thighs were spread.

Then he was in bed beside her with his hands all over her tits. It was like he had never seen tits in real life before.

"You can suck them if you want," Irene said.

He was kneeling on the bed beside her and bent his head down, holding one large breast in both his hands. He began sucking that breast and then took both breasts in his hands and brought her nipples together so that he could suck them both at the same time. The feeling was intense.

The sensation of his hands kneading her boobs rhythmically coupled with the intensity of his sucking on her rigid nipples brought feelings of pleasure floating through her. He switched back to sucking on one breast.

She reached up with one of her hands and began to play with her other nipple, pinching it and pulling it.

It felt like both nipples reached down to her clit as if a thin strand of nerve endings connected these three points off her sexuality.

Irene then moved her hand to his cock and pulled it as if to guide him between her legs. He moved, barely releasing her breast except to readjust his angle of attack. He was still sucking ferociously as he entered her.

The well hung lad had a little trouble squeezing his cock into Irene. She had not thought to bring any lubrication because she always seemed to be wet and she was sure that her wetness would accommodate any eventuality that she encountered this evening.

The young fellow seem to grasp that it was a tight fit and he pulled his cock and to the entrance of her vagina and then moved to forward an inch and back out and back in.

Then he reached down and took his cock in his hand and held it as he pulled it to the opening to her cunt. He rubbed his penis tip along her vagina lubricating it with his own liquids. She was damper now and he tried once more. This time he heard the soft pop as he tried once again to insert his full 10 inches deep into Irene.

Meanwhile, Carla was on her third guy. The first guy had done fine job in pleasuring her. The second had only lasted a couple of strokes. He explained that the excitement of watching his buddy fuck Carla had brought him to the bursting point even before the first one finished.

Carla had not been aware that the guys were sneaking in and watching her fuck. That's when Carla made the unilateral decision to move all potential studs out of the room.

They could not watch from outside but they could listen from outside. There was no need for them to be brought to the point of near climax before they entered her domain.

Remaking the Plan

When Irene and Carla got home after their night at the frat house, they were exhausted but neither of them actually knew where to start talking about what had gone wrong.

Irene wanted to have some sleep first but she also realized that sleep would improve her mood and she might lose some of the edge. She looked at Carla and said, "So how was that for you?"

Carla said, "I can see by the look on your face that you know exactly how I feel because I feel exactly the way you feel."

"What bothers me the most," Irene said, "Is that I think it was our fault."

Carla groaned.

Irene said, "I know. I know. Self blame is a useless exercise. And the worst part is, I'm not even sure what went wrong."

"It felt like work." Carla started putting on a pot of coffee, slamming the coffee can down on the counter and turning on the tap for water. "It wasn't fun."

Irene, who had fantasized about having serial sex, knew exactly what Carla meant. It was work.

Irene said, "What really pisses me off, was that we ended up entertaining a bunch of brats –."

"Frat brats." Carla said.

Irene laughed. It felt good to laugh and she knew that she laughed more than the comment deserved but it helped restore some balance in her mind.

Irene said, "It was like we had fine wine and they were drinking it out of paper cups."

Then she had a sudden insight. "You know, there is some good news. Not too long ago we would have considered ourselves lucky to have anybody pay attention to us. Never mind wait in line for our attention."

Carla agreed. She thought it was interesting how their attitudes were changing. She always sought male attention, at least in her mind. She was too shy in real life to reach out to a man, or to flirt with a man, or to expect a man to notice her.

"You have a point. But one of the things that bothers me is – well just like you said, fine wine and paper cups. They didn't appreciate us. They put no effort into it at all."

Carla pressed the button for the coffee. "I've learned that a guy doesn't have to last really long or even have a huge cock to participate in a good piece of tail. But they have to at least pretend to be putting more effort into it then they would if they were just going to have a beer."

The women sat and drank coffee and talked about the events of the night before. Irene took a couple of sips of her coffee and asked, "Is this decaf?"

Carla said, "No." It was three o'clock in the morning but both women had lost sense of time. They had started partying at 10 and took their first break at midnight.

They started the proceedings again around one but by that time most of the frat boys were either passed out or too drunk to be entertaining. The girls had unceremoniously gathered up their clothes and come home.

Each of them showered and washed their hair. They tossed their clothes in the laundry basket. They reeked of tobacco, marijuana, and stale beer.

On the way home both of them were exhausted and Irene had been thinking about how good her bed was going to feel. After she showered and got the smell of the frat house off her, she began to think about what disappointment it had been.

This was like attending a seminar. She felt she was doing a wrap up of her experiences. What was your take away from this workshop?

She talked to Carla about the possibility that perhaps there was some value in the night. They had a good idea, the notion of doing auditions.

Carla said "Well, that was our goal and what we learned was that…."

"Exactly. What we learned was that we should be more diligent with our auditions. A couple of those guys should've been weeded out of the line before they got to us."

They had no immediate answers to the big question which was, what went wrong? The girls felt some satisfaction in knowing that it was equally disappointing for both of them.

They were frustrated in not being able to figure out what went wrong.

A New Approach

There was another party two nights later. Most of the fraternity members were in the engineering department. Irene had been about to say that perhaps they would be more sensible when she remembered that the previous and disastrous frat party had been mostly business students.

She reminded herself that she was jumping to conclusions and making generic assessments of people based on stereotypes.

She of all people knew that stereotypes were a poor basis for judging people. She had an inkling of an old and annoying feeling at that moment.

It was a feeling that whipped her back to her high school years. The stereotype that touched her then was the stereotype that fat girls would put out because they were so grateful for attention.

She wondered briefly if the reason she felt the anger after the frat party had anything to do with that. Were these boys so bad in bed because they felt they did not put any extra effort in because they were screwing up a couple of fat broads.

Even when she thought that phrase – "fat broad" – Irene could feel the quotation marks around it. She hated those words and just thinking of them made her slightly depressed.

She wondered if there was any point in going to another party. What if it was just gang of frat boys just like the last ones.

Carla was the one who came up with the idea of being more demanding. "Aside from everything else," Carla said, "I think it be good for us, you and me, to learn how to set standards for these guys.

"You mean something to make them drop their drawers and produce an impressive hard on?"

"No. That's a physical attribute they can't do anything about. Sure I think given a choice I'd prefer a big cock but I don't like eliminating anybody based on their physical appearance."

Irene cringed. She had never thought of it that way. Here she could bitch and complain about anybody using the phrase fat broad around her but she was perfectly willing to judge other people on something that was beyond their control.

This of course led her into thinking about the control issue. One of the reasons that any reference to her weight had always bothered her is that everybody who wasn't plump seem to think that somehow it was a character flaw to be fat. Like they couldn't control themselves.

Luckily, Carla interrupted her before she went too far down this line of thought. "I was thinking more along the lines off making them do something for us before we did anything for them."

Always practical, Irene said, "Well we could make them go down on us I suppose and show a little technique but that could be difficult. For the first guy be fine but after that we'd be a little bit too juicy."

"That's something else – that's kind of creepy. The whole notion of sloppy seconds. I think we're going to have to take more time of each encounter and douche in between. I mean, I did six guys in a row."

Irene nodded agreement. "We do need to have a little more control over the event. Like each guy gets half an hour. If he blows his wad in two minutes, that's his problem not ours. Especially if we make him come up with some way to pleasure us first."

Carla was quiet and then she said in a low voice, "It's a sad statement on our self-esteem that we had to figure these things out. I keep thinking of Marianne back in high school. I used to be in one of those situations where someone was taking advantage of me and I'd wonder, what would Marianne do?"

Irene and Carla had only met in the second year of university and they had rarely discussed their high school days with each other. But Irene knew exactly what Carla was talking about.

Curvy Girls Do It Collection
9 Complete Erotic Romance Stories

There was a girl in her high school that Irene used to think about in exactly the same way. What would Jennifer do?

Irene said, "I know what you mean. And the worst thing is I used to tell myself that it was more important to be nice than anything else."

Carla said, "Being nice is important but not if being nice means letting your buddy use you like a doormat."

The two women commiserated with each other about mistakes they had made in their approach to life in the past. This solidified the new plan for the next frat party. Basically, they would be a pair of bitches.

The Frat Party

Subconsciously, both women had started to dress better. It wasn't that they went shopping for new outfits. They just dug into the back of their closets and found things that they had never worn.

Irene found clothes that she had been saving for special occasions. She had to laugh at herself. What would constitute a special occasion in her life?

Well, maybe the frat party they were going to tonight would be considered a special occasion but the memory of the last frat party still clung to her and she found it hard to think of anything special about a bunch of horny guys who were selfish beyond belief.

Carla looked fabulous in a deep green sleeveless dress that showed off her blonde hair and brought out shades of blue and green in her eyes. She was wearing gold sandals.

Irene said, "Those nice shoes. I've never seen those before. Are they new?" She had to smile at herself. In her entire life, she had never enthused about somebody else's footwear. It was definitely the dawn of a new day in Irene's life.

Irene was wearing deep purple leggings with a silver brocade pattern tunic. The tunic was long enough that she could've worn it as a dress if she had been accustomed to showing that much of her body in public.

Irene had braided her long hair in a single braid that hung down her back. When they showed up at the frat house, the president met them at the door and shook their hands.

He was tall and muscular and extremely handsome. Handsome with movie star good looks. Irene gave him a cool, measured smile. She was going to role-play being a bitch. At least as far as she could understand being a bitch.

There were other women at the party and Irene was surprised. Somehow she hadn't expected women to be there. She had to remind herself that she was as elegant and as nicely turned out as any of them.

As she and Carla were being shown to the bedrooms that they would be using, Irene had an idea. She turned to Carla and said, "I just thought of something. Carla, what about if we did it in the same room."

Carla frowned at her quizzically.

"I was thinking that if we were both in the same room with two beds, we could make sure that each of us have a good time."

Irene was not explaining it properly. Part of it was that she knew that she gained strength from Carla's presence. Besides she had been somewhat titillated watching the first guy at the last party mount Carla. She hadn't thought of it until now.

But that was not the main reason. She got strength from Carla's presence and she could be more daring in ordering a man to do what she wanted.

Such as telling him what to do when he had his tongue on her clit. Or if he stuck one long skinny finger in her wet cunt. Two fingers or even three fingers would be more pleasurable for her.

One finger could be annoying, but that was just based on an experience she had at the last frat party. She probably would've been annoyed at whatever the young men had done.

Carla said, "I think that's a good idea. And that way we can signal each other earlier if it becomes another one of those tedious nights where I feel like I'm working or you feel like you're working."

"We're dangerously close to being working girls as it is," Irene said.

"Exactly." Carla said. "We just lost track of the main point which was for you and me to have a good time."

Carla wondered if perhaps they had been spoiled by beginning their sexual adventures with rock stars.

Going downhill to a bunch of immature college boys was bound to be a letdown. But then she thought of Paul and Scott. That had been a really good experience.

The new plan worked out fairly well. The evening evolved gradually and the evolution began when the first guy came into the bedroom that had two double beds separated by about eight feet of carpet.

Carla was sitting on the edge of her bed and Irene was standing when the guy entered the room. He closed the door. He was just under six feet tall and had short cropped hair, broad shoulders, narrow hips and an arrogant tilt to his head.

Irene speculated that perhaps he was just a little bit nervous. "I'm Irene," she said.

"Brad."

Carla said, "Nice to meet you Brad."

Brad stood, uncertain which woman he was supposed to be with. Irene was about to ask him to choose one of them and realize instantly that was the wrong approach.

"Get over here." She indicated her bed. He moved toward the bed and sat down. Irene continued, "Strip. Take it all off."

She was amused at how easily he started obeying her. Brad began to undress, taking off his shoes and socks first. Then his shirt and his jeans and finally his underpants.

Irene was surprised to see that his cock was already turgid. His balls were tucked up tight and a tip of his penis glistened. He was pretty excited and if he was already having first few drops of his cum dribble out of him, he would likely not last more than a minute.

Well, he would have to work a little before his ejaculation was permitted. "Now undress me," she commanded.

Brad stood up and walked toward her. He hesitated and Irene could tell that he wasn't sure where to start. She gave him a couple of seconds to see if he would move toward her with some indication of whether he was going to start with her tunic or her leggings.

When he didn't move she said, "Take off my top."

He reached for her tunic and tugged it up and over her head. It wasn't easy for him but he carried off the job fairly well.

Irene was wearing one of her new bras that covered her double D tits in a way that maximized her cleavage. Brad reached around her which brought him so close to her that her tits were pressed up against his naked and hairy chest.

He unhooked her bra and guided the straps down over her arms letting her girls fall loose. They were particularly pendulous and Irene saw his excitement as he stared at them once they were set free.

He was almost salivating.

"You may kiss them," Irene said. He leaned down and kissed the tops of both breasts and then moved to her nipples which were now sticking out like big pencil erasers.

He flicked one with the fingers of his left hand while he cupped her right breast in his other hand and took her nipple in his mouth. The flick surprised her, both because he did it and because it gave her a shot that felt like liquid electricity.

He was very good at this. Irene didn't want him to stop. He nuzzled and nibbled and sucked and Irene could feel herself getting damp.

Carla said, "The next guy can wait. I'm going to continue to observe." She knew she was speaking to a room where no one was listening to her but she didn't care.

They had discussed how this would work. Carla was enjoying the scene before her. It was making her extremely horny to watch her friend having her enormous tits played with.

Carla's own tits were as flat as fried eggs but they were extremely sensitive. She had from time to time been able to bring herself off simply from playing with her own nipples.

She was tempted to play with them now but she thought it would be more intense to let the feelings wash over her. Then when her partner showed up, she would be ready to command him to play with her nipples.

She hoped he had the stamina to last beyond a couple of strokes because she would only need a few strokes to reach an orgasm that she knew would be earth shattering.

Irene was guiding Brad to the bed and she told him to remove her pants and underpants. He peeled them off in one smooth motion.

Irene adjusted herself so that she was on the bed, lying spread-eagled using her arms to hold her breasts upright on her chest. Brad climbed between her legs and took her breasts in his hands again.

"Oh my God," he said, "you have the most beautiful tits I've ever seen. You are beautiful."

Then his hands still on her tits, he moved his cock up and sank into Irene's nest.

Carla watched his ass muscles expand and contract as he pulled back and thrust forward. Irene began to moan and then said, "Oh yes, oh yes." She was moving her hips in unison with Brad.

Brad's ass muscles contracted tightly and he stopped moving. He was trying to hold his orgasm back. Anyone could see that but his attempt to hold back was too late.

Suddenly he began moving hard and fast and he roared almost as if he were in pain as he dumped his load into Irene.

Carla grinned to herself. She'd give him an eight out of 10. She wished she had a paddle that she could hold up with the number eight.

The Judges Talk

After Brad redressed himself and left the room, Irene turned to Carla and said, "Thanks for going along with that."

"You mean watching? It was my pleasure." Then she told Irene about the thought of having the paddle that she could hold up to show her judgment of Brad's performance. She told Irene she would've given him an eight.

Irene said, "I would have to. He was pretty good. That is the kind of sex that I want to have. And I got to tell you I'm ready for more."

This was the feeling she had had where one orgasm wasn't enough. She knew that she could handle more fucking right away.

"Are you going to watch me?" Carla asked.

"If you don't mind. I'll hold up my imaginary paddle at the end and give you my score."

And so that was how the evening went. The women took turns ordering the men to please them and they took their time between encounters to freshen up and rearrange themselves.

Once More?

The girls needed a rest after their evening with the engineers. Irene got a call the next afternoon from the president of the engineering frat house.

"I just want to thank you ladies for coming to our party last night. I'm sorry I didn't have a chance to get to know you better," he said.

Irene responded with the appropriate pleasantries. The old Irene would have asked him what he wanted or found some way to find out rather than wait for him to speak again.

That was the old Irene. The new Irene waited.

Finally he said, "A few of us guys are having a private party next week and we would like to invite you and Carla to attend."

"How big a party is it?" Irene asked.

He said, "Six." She could hear the question in his voice.

Irene got the details from him and informed him that they may bring another friend or two with them.

Peggy and Michaela joined them in the party which started out as a cocktail party at the house of one of the men. Irene realized that not all the men were frat boys. Two of them were older and it was one of the older men who owned the house. They were not ancient, but they were closer to forty than to thirty.

It was a spacious and gracious house with many small rooms and lots of mirrored surfaces. Peggy and Michaela had come to the girls' apartment early so that they could talk about some of their experiences over the past couple of weeks.

Peggy said, "I'm really glad you invited me. I was afraid that I'd never get a chance again to play like we played that night with the rock stars."

Carla said, "Men are always horny. They'll always be there to play with."

Peggy said, "Yes but where do you find them? The only place I ever see men is at work and I just cannot get up the courage to even hint at anything there. And if I did, they would misunderstand."

Irene and Carla laughed at that comment because they had felt the same way. They explained to Peggy that they felt the same way.

Carla added, "I've already had more sex than I ever thought I'd have in my whole life." Then she admitted that maybe she was exaggerating a little.

"The point is," Irene said, "We're finally getting enough. Well, I am."

Michaela sighed, "Sounds great to me."

They had a glass of wine and Irene explained to the two new girls that there were six men and only four of them. So the logistics would be interesting.

Irene was quick to point out that they did not have to do anything they did not want to do. Carla piped up, "It is supposed to be fun."

They took a taxi to the party and Irene could see that Peggy was impressed by the house and the men. None of the men were guys she recognized from the frat party, except for the president of the fraternity.

His name was Jeremiah and the five men were friends of his from outside the fraternity and the two older men were professors at the university.

Peggy was cozied up to one of the older men almost immediately, smiling coyly up at him. He leaned down and kissed her.

Irene looked around to see Michaela with the other older man and one of the younger men. She was sitting in a big arm chair and each man was sitting on the floor beside her.

They were taking her shoes off and Irene grinned as the older man lifted her foot to his mouth and began to suck her toes.

She couldn't see Carla. Nor could she see the other two men. That left her with Jeremiah. He was handsome but part of Irene was envious that Carla was with two men. In her typical analytical fashion, Irene wondered why she would want quantity when she had quality right here in front of her.

She knew that all of these men were quality fucks and clearly knew more than the typical frat boy.

"You're tense," Jeremiah said. He put his capable hands on her neck and began to massage her neck.

She said, "Just feel like I have to keep an eye on the girls."

He said, "Well, let's do that. We are in charge here. Let's see what the others are doing."

He led her to the den that was off to the left of the living room. Peggy and her professor were humping on the sofa, his pale ass moving to the beat of the rock music that was playing in the room.

Jeremiah said, "They look occupied." He took her hand and led her to the next room which was a large bedroom, with a large bed. Carla was naked on the bed, her eyes closed and a huge smile on her face as the older man pleasured her between her legs.

The younger man was tickling her little breasts with a gigantic feather, running the end of it over her erect nipples.

Irene said to Jeremiah, "She is crazy about having her nipples pinched and sucked."

He looked at Irene and then at Carla. "Well, the only gentlemanly thing to do is to give her what she wants. He moved to the bed, dropping his clothes as he went. Irene followed.

It was a king sized bed. As Irene sat beside her friend, the man who had been licking Carla lifted his head and moved away from Carla. The feather-tickler laid the feather down on the night table and moved to Carla's cunt.

Jeremiah squeezed one of Carla's nipples between his fingers while he gently bit the other nipple. The professor stroked Irene and she knew this was the start of something very good.